Phoenix Langrish

A woman who made the world stand still.

At eighteen she had been beautiful. At twenty-eight she was stunning. And she did something to Nash Vallender's heart that no other woman had ever been capable of.

Unaware of being watched, she closed the car door, and dropped the notebook she was carrying. Bending to pick it up, she dropped her bag, and as she straightened, the small camera she was carrying around her neck caught on the door handle. Still clumsy. Still so very lovable.

She gave a husky little laugh, closed her eyes, took a deep breath, untangled the camera and turned.

Never had a smile been wiped away so quickly, he thought as she glared at him in shock.

"Hello, Phoenix." He greeted her quietly, and his voice was husky, as husky as it had been all those years before.

Dear Reader,

Get ready to meet the world's most eligible bachelors: they're sexy, successful and, best of all, they're all yours!

This month in **Harlequin Romance®** we bring you the latest in our great new series **Bachelor Territory**. A series of six books with two things in common—they're all predominantly written from the hero's point of view and they're absolutely wonderful!

This month's book is *One Bride Required!* by Emma Richmond. In July look out for Heather Allison's latest Romance, written under her real name of Heather MacAllister. It's a name you're sure to recognize, as Heather MacAllister is one of the leading lights in our Harlequin Temptation® series.

Happy reading!

The Editors

BACHELOR
TERRITORY

*There are two sides to every story...
and now it's his turn!*

One Bride Required!

Emma Richmond

Harlequin Books

TORONTO • NEW YORK • LONDON
AMSTERDAM • PARIS • SYDNEY • HAMBURG
STOCKHOLM • ATHENS • TOKYO • MILAN
MADRID • WARSAW • BUDAPEST • AUCKLAND

ISBN 0-373-03505-5

ONE BRIDE REQUIRED!

First North American Publication 1998.

Printed in U.S.A.

CHAPTER ONE

NASH VALLENDER hadn't known he was a hero, or not until quite recently, that was. Not, in fact, until he'd taken leave of his senses. Leaning on the sagging gate, his dark hair ruffled by the May breeze, grey eyes rueful, he stared at the derelict ruin in front of him.

Oddly Manor. Oddly named, oddly listing to one side, and, even more oddly, his. A distant aunt, one he barely remembered, had left it to him. Because he was brave. He hadn't understood what the executor of her will had meant at the time. He did now. Not the bravery of fighting dragons, but of withstanding bombardment and sabotage. He'd been blitzed with letters and visits from the villagers begging him to keep and restore it. Driven nearly insane with the unwanted persistence of the developers to encourage him to offload it onto them as though he should be grateful for such generosity. The executors had made veiled references to the untold pressure put on his *aunt* to sell. In fact everyone, except the villagers, was of the same opinion. Get rid of it. Which he should have done.

He wasn't philanthropic, he wasn't a romantic, and he had certainly never overly concerned himself about the fate of the English countryside, but he did have a strong aversion to being pressurised. Which was why, having thwarted the developers' dream of turning the land into an estate of mock Tudor homes, thus becoming a knight in shining armour to the villagers of Mincott Oddly, where his bequest stood, he was now standing in the May sunshine viewing his very own ruin and wondering what on earth he was going to do with it.

But if someone considered you brave, he thought with a small self-mocking smile, even if it was only a distant, barely remembered, now dead relative, there was somehow a compulsion not to prove them wrong. A compulsion that was going to prove very costly. Not only the renovation, but trying to find out who was so busily trying to destroy the house. Because someone was.

Windows were broken; slates fell from the roof with alarming regularity; small fires broke out due to defective wiring—or so he had been told. A coping stone had narrowly missed injuring one of the villagers who was keeping an eye on the place. The obvious contenders for the sabotage were, of course, the developers. But he had no proof. Which was why he had rung a private detective he'd used before and left a message on his answering machine. Hopefully he would get back to him some time soon.

He glanced sadly at the ivy that was slowly strangling the stonework, and the definitely sagging roof of the east wing. Although why it was called the east wing he had no idea. The whole *house* faced east. But that was what the executors had called it, and no doubt that was what it would remain. He really should have sold. Building land was at a premium again. He could have asked, and probably got, over two hundred thousand for it. He was one of the most respected businessmen in London, and he was behaving like a fool. Never in a million years would he have thought he'd want to hold onto a mouldering pile that was only good for knocking down. But it had ten acres. So did Nettlesham Swamp, he told himself with a grin, but that didn't mean anyone in their right mind would want to keep it! And for a man who had taken on multinational corporations and won, taken on white-water rapids on nothing more substantial than a boat resembling a banana leaf, trying to persuade himself to look on it as a challenge, and not the white elephant it undoubtedly was, was even more foolish.

His friends thought him mad, including Mike, his architect, who was supposed to be looking over the property and who seemed to have disappeared. His enemies thought him a fool, but he didn't explain and he didn't try to justify himself—a policy that had stood him in good stead in the past. Whether it would stand him in good stead now, he didn't know; he only knew that few people would ever understand why he had behaved as he had. But then, people very rarely understood him. Never understood the risks he took in business or in his leisure. He wasn't entirely sure he understood them either. Just the way he was made, he supposed. And opposition always made him stubborn. In business that was sometimes a good thing, because his stubbornness was usually based on knowledge, insight, but in this instance his stubbornness was based on—what? A whim? No, because if the developers hadn't come, hadn't tried to pressurise him, he would probably have sold. And he would then never have had the perfect opportunity to meet someone he hadn't seen in a very long time.

Glancing at his watch, he gave a rueful smile. He couldn't remember the last time he had waited for someone with such expectation. How much had she changed? he wondered. How much had *he* changed?

Hearing a car, he stilled. Listening intently, he plotted the car's movements by sound alone. He couldn't see it, any more than the driver could see him, because of the high, untrimmed hedges, but if she parked where she'd been instructed to park... For a man of such courage, he mocked himself, he was feeling an odd reluctance to actually face her. Not that any of his thoughts showed on his face. They never did.

Lifting the gate in order to open it, he walked round the side of the house to stare at the small blue car that had just parked.

Ten years ago he and the woman inside that car had almost had an affair, but she'd been due to go up to university and he'd had the chance to go to the States, something he'd very much wanted to do. 'Wrong time, wrong place,' he'd told her gently. 'Go and carve out your career.' She hadn't begged, pleaded, had just looked at him, then walked away. It hadn't been easy to let her go, and a large part of him had always regretted it, and so, when the opportunity had come to see her again...

Fate? he wondered. Preordained? He had no idea, but just before he had learned of his bequest he'd seen an article about her, about house-detecting. About how she tried to discover the origins of old houses. When the Manor had come into his hands it had seemed the most natural thing in the world to write and ask her to come and see him.

Except she didn't know it was to be him. He'd asked the executor of his aunt's will to write to her, to make the arrangements without mentioning his name. And he shouldn't have done that. But if she'd known who she was really coming to see she wouldn't have come—might not have come. And perhaps that would have been best. You couldn't go back, re-create the past, no matter how much you might want to. Too late now.

The car door finally opened, and a woman slowly emerged.

Phoenix Langrish.

A woman who made the world stand still.

At eighteen, she had been beautiful. At twenty-eight she was stunning. And she did something to his heart that no other woman had ever been capable of. Not because she was beautiful, because beauty only temporarily stirred the senses. This was something more.

Delicate and feminine, with long dark hair held back in a clip that was inadequate to the task, wide brown eyes and a mouth that was made to smile.

Unaware of being watched, she closed the car door and dropped the notebook she was carrying.

Bending to pick it up, she dropped her bag, and as she straightened the small camera she was carrying around her neck caught on the door handle. Still clumsy. Still so very lovable.

She gave a husky little laugh, closed her eyes, took a deep breath, untangled the camera, and turned.

Never had a smile been wiped away so quickly, he thought, as she glared at him in shock. She was rooted to the spot, and her eyes widened until they could widen no more. She didn't speak, just stood there, looking at him.

'Hello, Phoenix,' he greeted her quietly, and his voice was husky. As husky as it had been all those years before.

'No,' she whispered. Turning abruptly away, she trod in a rut, staggered, and caught the wing mirror for support. It came off in her hand.

She stared at it, just stared, as though she didn't know what it was, and then she shuddered, tried to pull herself together. She reached for the car door; he reached it first.

'Don't leave.'

Her breathing unnatural, she looked at him. 'You...I...'

'Yes. I didn't tell you it would be me meeting you because I didn't think you would come. And I wanted you to.'

She didn't answer. Perhaps she couldn't. Just continued to stare at him.

As he stared at her. As he had all those years before in a crowded hotel foyer. Ten years had changed nothing. Even in an ill-fitting suit that looked as though it might have belonged to someone with a larger build she set his senses on fire. She'd had a wild freedom then, an exuberance for life. Awkward, enthusiastic, and totally without guile. Now she looked frightened, caged.

'I find I don't know what to say to you,' he said quietly.

'Goodbye?' she proffered huskily.

'No,' he denied gently. 'Come and see the house.'

Taking her silence for an affirmative, which he knew it wasn't, he removed the wing mirror from her hand, opened the car door and tossed it inside.

'No,' she argued hoarsely. 'I...'

'Please?' Holding her arm, feeling the shivers that ran through her, the electric tension that he controlled rather better than she did, he led her round to the front of the house. Aware of every little breath she took, every little move she made, he asked, 'What do you think of it?'

She didn't answer, merely stared unseeingly at the house in front of them.

Turning his head, he slowly examined her exquisite profile, and, resisting the almost overwhelming impulse to touch that thick dark hair, he murmured, 'Is it worth restoring, do you think?'

'I don't know.'

Unable to take his eyes off her, he put one hand over hers, and she jumped nervously. 'I am sorry, Phoenix.'

Finally turning her head, she looked at him, and it was as if a shutter came down over her eyes, hiding her thoughts, her feelings from him. 'Are you?'

'Yes.'

'For what?'

'The deception.'

She nodded, made an obvious effort to pull herself together, and returned her attention to the house.

'So, what do you think?'

'I don't know. You'd need a structural engineer to tell you that. All I can tell you is what things are.'

'Then tell me what they are.'

'Why?' she demanded raggedly. 'Why now?'

'Because I saw an article about you, and I suddenly found that I wanted to see you again.'

She gave a bitter smile. 'And never mind that I might not have wanted to be seen?'

'Didn't you?'

'I don't know,' she said helplessly.

'It would be a lucrative commission...'

'That isn't why you invited me.'

'No, I was curious. Didn't you know that curiosity was my besetting sin? And you're even more beautiful now than you were then.'

'Thank you,' she said without inflexion. With an abrupt movement away from him, she announced baldly, 'I'm going home.'

Halting her, he asked, 'Not even a little bit curious to see what's inside? The article said it was your passion...'

'So were you,' she retorted without thinking, 'and look what that got me.'

'A degree,' he answered. 'A life. It wouldn't have worked, Phoenix. Not then.'

'No,' she agreed.

'And I never meant to hurt you.'

'I know you didn't.'

They both stared at the house in silence.

'The article said you were making quite a name for yourself,' he finally murmured. 'I'm glad.'

'Thank you.'

Such a flat little voice, devoid of meaning, but he could feel the tension in her. Feel it in himself.

'Shall we go in?' Leading the way up the weed-choked path, hoping she would follow, he pushed open the heavy front door. 'Will you at least look round? Give me your honest opinion?'

She looked suddenly helpless and distracted. 'Don't come with me.'

'All right. Don't go in the bedrooms in the east wing,' he cautioned. 'One of the ceilings is down and the roof is unsafe.'

Without answering, she walked quickly away to the left of the grand staircase. He wanted to follow, unobserved, wanted to see what she was doing, how she was behaving now that he was no longer beside her.

Long after she was out of sight, with only the sound of her high heels tapping on the bare boards, he remained where he was, his feelings ambivalent. He hadn't been *quite* prepared for the sensations he'd experienced when she'd stepped from the car. Wasn't entirely prepared for them now. An overwhelming feeling of belonging. But what was she like now? After her initial shock, she had given nothing away of her personality. At eighteen she had been vivacious, laughing, loving. What was she now? Never one to rush his fences, even if his feelings *were* urging action, he would allow her time and space to make up her own mind. If he could.

In the meantime, he thought with a rather twisted smile, he would make his own tour, maybe go and look at his very own entablature. Not that he was entirely sure what it was, only that the executor had assured him that he had one. He'd looked it up, but being told that it was the top part of an architectural order, which consisted of horizontal mouldings, hadn't been very enlightening.

But his mind was on Phoenix as he slowly climbed the grand staircase. Remembering *not* to grasp the handrail, which had a tendency to wobble alarmingly, he turned left at the small landing where the staircase divided, climbed the further five steps that led to the landing proper, and which ran on either side to the front of the house, and ambled aimlessly through the warren of bedrooms and one antiquated bathroom. He took a brief look into the east wing to make sure no further damage had occurred, then found the small back staircase that went down to the rabbit warren of rooms that had once presumably housed the scullery, dairy and kitchen, and which would definitely need major remodification.

Returning to the top of the staircase, he headed in the opposite direction, into rooms that interconnected. Perhaps they'd once been the nursery. One room for Nanny, one for the child and one for playing in, or taking tea in front of a roaring fire. No sign of it now, of course—even the fire surround had been removed. By whom? he wondered. But it was only an absent thought because his mind was still on Phoenix.

As he walked into the room at the front, a small smile tugged at his mouth as he stared up at the ornate cornice. 'Behold,' he murmured softly, 'one entablature. I probably have several others, of course... And talking to yourself is the first sign of madness. Or is it the second?' But then, he was mad, wasn't he? To take on this monstrosity. Some of the rooms were damp. Most were inhabitable... He should have sold. It was going to cost an absolute fortune to restore. But the view had to be almost worth it, he decided as he stared from the window. Open fields, hedgerows, coppices, and, in the foreground, the quaint and rather delightful village of Mincott Oddly. Crooked cottages around an ancient green.

What was she doing now? He could hear no sounds from the rest of the house. Was she thinking about him? A small conceit, he thought wryly; she might not be thinking about him at all. But he wanted her to be. Wanted her to feel as he was feeling. An ache in the loins, a heady feeling of adventure.

Fool, he scolded himself. But wasn't it allowed to be a fool just once in your life? Twice, he mentally corrected. He'd been a fool ten years ago.

Shaking off his introspection, because thinking about it did him absolutely no good at all, and intending to go and look for Mike, he was momentarily distracted by the sight of a small door on his right. He'd always assumed it was a cupboard, but, opening it, he found a short flight of stairs, which of course had to be investigated. Climbing carefully, on treads that felt decidedly rickety beneath his weight, he opened the door at the top and peered into the cavernous space beneath the roof. Too dark to see anything clearly, and probably infested by spiders. He carefully retreated and made his way back to the landing.

Hearing minuscule scratching sounds, he looked over the banister and saw Phoenix, delicately picking plaster from his walls. For a long, long moment he watched her, unobserved. Her face was intent, but rather sad, he thought.

'What are you doing?' he asked softly.

Startled, she looked up guiltily, and, cursing himself for a fool, knowing what was about to happen, he swung himself over the railing, dropped lightly down to the half-landing, and was just in time to prevent her stumbling backwards down the staircase.

'Sorry,' he apologised, his breathing barely altered. 'I didn't mean to frighten you.'

'No. I mean, it's all right. No damage done.'

'Except to the plaster,' he said drily. 'I thought the whole idea was to put plaster *on* the walls, not take it off.'

'Yes. It was already cracked,' she excused hastily. 'I mean, I didn't... You could have broken your neck jumping like that.'

'Nonsense, I'm incredibly fit,' he boasted mockingly. 'So, what were you doing?'

With a sigh that sounded despairing, she murmured, 'I just wanted to see what was underneath.'

Eyes gentle, he asked, 'And what is?'

'I don't know, but...'

'Then look.' Inserting his fingernail beneath a flake of plaster, he pulled it free. 'Looks like an old window.'

When she didn't immediately answer, he turned to look at her, and was astonished to see shock, almost awed bewilderment on her lovely face as she stared at what he had exposed.

'Oh, my,' she whispered reverently as she

reached out to pull off another, larger piece of plaster. 'It can't be.'

Amused, he asked, 'What can't?'

'Bar tracery.'

'Why can't it?' he asked, with absolutely no idea what bar tracery was.

'Because it can't.'

'Why?'

'Sorry?'

Lips twitching, he queried, '*What* is bar tracery?'

'This. I need to look outside.' With an abrupt movement that took him by surprise, she began haring down the stairs, and nearly mowed down a tall, thin gentleman, who was just crossing the hall at the bottom.

'Whoa,' he laughed.

'Sorry,' she apologised hastily. With a fleeting smile, she continued out through the front door.

'Who was *that*?' Mike exclaimed in astonished appreciation.

Face bland, Nash murmured, 'My house detective. I have bar tracery.' With a muffled laugh, and not waiting for any further comment, he continued after Phoenix, but, if he didn't miss his guess, his architect would be following close behind.

'Don't you want to know who that was?' he teased gently as he caught her up.

She halted so suddenly that he nearly knocked her over. 'What?' she asked blankly.

'The man in the hall.'

'Oh. Who was it?' she asked obediently.

'My architect.'

'Well, I wouldn't let him make recommendations until the house has been investigated properly.'

'No,' he agreed. 'He's just looking.'

She nodded, halted at the back of the house, and looked up.

Following her gaze, not at all sure what he was supposed to be looking at, he finally proffered, 'A bricked-up window?'

'Yes.'

'And is that good?' he asked as he turned to smile at the architect, who *had* followed them.

A reciprocal smile on his thin, humorous face, Mike also glanced upwards.

'Good?' she queried. '*Good?* It's Decorated *Gothic!*'

'Ah.'

'It's the most... I can't believe it. Oh, I can't believe it,' she whispered, her eyes still fixed on the window.

'Does that mean you'll stay?'

But she wasn't listening. 'Hardly any of them have survived,' she breathed. 'Or only in cathedrals. Lincoln and Carlisle, Melrose Abbey, York Minster. You'll need to hack the interior plaster off very, very carefully, of course, but you can see from here that the stonework is much narrower, and in "bars". See how the window area is much larger and wider, and encompassed by an equilateral arch?'

'Yes,' he agreed, his eyes on her beautiful profile.

'Divided vertically by stone mullions, it gives five, seven or even nine lights. Mid-fourteenth century.' Turning, only to find him staring at her instead of the window, she looked hastily away. 'You haven't instructed any builders…?'

'No,' he denied. 'I don't, as yet, have any builders.'

'Good. Only it's very important…'

'Not to disturb anything?' he said.

'Yes.' Looking anywhere but at him, she murmured, 'Perhaps you ought to think about getting the Manor listed.'

'No,' he said, because he knew very well that if it was listed *nothing* would be allowed to be done.

'But Inigo Jones might—'

'No,' he interrupted softly.

'You don't know who he is,' she accused.

'Was.'

Mike laughed. 'Give in,' he urged his friend. 'You appear to have met your match, and I have to go. Nice to have met you, Miss...?'

'Langrish,' Nash supplied helpfully as he steered Mike back towards the path, without allowing him to say anything further.

'Talk about "speed the parting guest",' he complained humorously. 'Not that I blame you; she's stunning!'

'Yes, she is. A phoenix who falls *into* the ashes rather than rises from them. That's her name,' he explained at Mike's frown.

'Oh.'

'She was born in a fire—well, not precisely, but there was a fire in the next-door apartment whilst her mother was in labour. She arrived just as the firemen were carrying out the stretcher.' And he wanted her with a fierce desire that was almost frightening. 'How knowledgeable is she?'

Halting again, Mike gave his friend a silent scrutiny before asking, 'Not sure about her?'

'I'm not sure about *anybody*. You have *heard* of bar tracery?' he queried lightly.

'Er...'

Nash laughed. 'Inigo Jones?'

'Now, that I *can* tell you. He was one of England's first great architects.'

'Professor Morton? She apparently trained under him.'

'Yes, and certainly *he's* reputable.'

'Good.'

'As if you didn't know.' Mike grinned. 'Knowing you as well as I do—or as well as anyone is ever likely to—I imagine you've checked her out down to what colour nail varnish she uses.'

'Was she wearing nail varnish?' Nash queried innocently. 'I didn't notice.'

'Liar.'

Reaching the gate, they both turned to stare at the Manor. 'Had the surveyor's report in yet?' asked Mike.

Nash shook his head.

'And will you live here when it's restored—*if* it's ever restored?'

'I don't know.'

'Heard from Chrissie?' he asked casually.

'No.'

'Mind my own business?'

'Mmm.'

With a faint smile, he strolled towards his car. 'Perhaps someone ought to tell her she has fierce competition,' he added slyly. 'Meanwhile, I'll get some ideas down on paper and let you have them in a few days. Let me know if you need a demolition expert,' he called back. 'Or a chaperon.'

As the car drove away, and with nothing of his thoughts showing on his face, Nash turned to see Phoenix picking her way back along the rutted path.

Reaching the front door, he was just in time to catch her as she tripped over the step. And he wanted to kiss her.

She moved hastily away from his supporting arm, avoided all eye contact.

'Still falling over, I see,' he murmured softly.

'Yes.' She didn't look awkward, or embarrassed about it, just accepting. Because she was so used to falling over things that it no longer held any importance? A fact of life, he wondered, like being left-handed?

'You should have worn flat shoes,' he reproved mildly.

'I know,' she agreed, her gaze fixed on the top of the staircase. 'I was interviewing the Mayoress and there wasn't time to change. I wonder why they covered it up?'

Momentarily off balance, he glanced at the wall at the top of the staircase and back to Phoenix. 'The window?'

'Yes.'

'Window tax?' he offered, not very knowl-
edgeably.

She shook her head. Opening her notebook,
fumbling for her glasses, which were hanging on
a cord round her neck, she began to write. 'I
won't touch anything else...'

'Won't you?' he asked softly. 'Pity.'

'Don't,' she said, her voice agitated. 'You'll
need to reveal the window.'

'You reveal it.'

'No, I...'

'You know you yearn to. Pretend I'm a
stranger. Pretend this is the first time we've met.
I wish it was,' he added.

'Don't,' she pleaded again.

Turning, she tried to brush past him. He easily
caught her, held her before him. 'Look at me,'
he ordered softly.

'No.' Struggling free, she took two steps back,
eyes still lowered.

'Why?'

'Because you aren't what you seem, Nash.
You never were.'

No, he wasn't what he seemed.

'You're ruthless and single-minded and you
wear the face of a fool.'

'A fool?' he queried softly.

'All right, a face of calmness and curiosity and

gentleness,' she substituted, almost crossly. 'And it's a lie. It was always a lie.'

'And that bothers you?'

'No,' she denied, obviously untruthfully.

'Good, but I really do need someone to tell me what I'm doing. Professor Morton will be cross if you don't,' he persuaded humorously when she didn't answer. 'And you won't have to see much of me.'

'I don't want to see anything of you.'

He gave a small smile for her petulance. 'You're a big girl now, Phoenix, surely capable of dealing with an old reprobate like me.'

Finally looking up, she asked quietly, 'Are you an old reprobate?'

'No,' he said. And every time he moved nearer she moved away. Eyes always averted. 'It would enhance your reputation,' he encouraged. 'And I don't imagine you find bar tracery every day of the week.'

'No.'

'Then why not take a stab at it? If you'd had anything else on you wouldn't have come here, would you? And jobs like this aren't exactly run-of-the-mill, are they?'

'No.'

Watching her for a moment, the way her hair fell over one shoulder, the soft curve of her mouth, he finally asked, 'Can we really not meet as friends? We're different people now. And no less aware of each other than we were ten years ago,' he added softly.

'Stop it,' she reproved, her face agitated. 'And if you expect to pick up where you left off...'

'I don't.' Would like to, he thought, and wasn't even surprised at how much he meant it. 'I'll pay you the going rate. I really do need your professional opinion on how to restore it.'

Conflicting emotions showing clearly on her face, professional interest against personal feelings, she glanced almost wistfully towards the hidden landing window.

'Think of the bar tracery,' he persuaded softly. 'Think of my entablatures.'

She gave a faint smile, and he felt unbelievably tender. And relieved. Never in his life to date had he ever had to persuade a woman to trust him. Neither had he wanted to. Until now.

'But do, please, try to remember,' he added, with a smile in his rather nice grey eyes, 'that I do need plaster on my walls. That I do need bedrooms, and bathrooms, and that historical artefacts must come second to *needs*. And do, for goodness' sake, take that camera from around your neck before you strangle yourself.'

Face still unsure, she unhooked the camera and put it into his waiting hand.

'Tell me why you were interviewing the Mayoress,' he invited. 'She has an old house that needs investigating?'

She shook her head. 'She was opening the children's ward at the hospital.'

Confused, amused, and really rather enjoying himself, he persisted, 'Then why were you interviewing her?'

'Because that's my other hat.'

'Your other hat?' he echoed.

'Yes.'

'*What* other hat?'

'Reporting. I don't earn very much as a house historian,' she murmured as she began to rub her hand over the old wood of the banister. 'Not very many people want to pay to be told they have Jacobean beams, or something. There aren't very many nobles inheriting castles without a documented history, and so I supplement my income by working for the local paper. Are you going to have the lawns relaid?'

'Don't change the subject,' he reproved. 'But, yes, I shall probably get them relaid.' Turning to glance briefly through the open front door at the scrubby grass that by no stretch of the imagination could be called lawn, he gave a rueful smile before turning back to Phoenix—who was half-way up the staircase.

A clear warning not to ask her personal questions? She was as nervous as a cat. 'Where are you going?' he asked as he followed her.

'Just checking something.' Taking the right fork, she halted on the top landing and stared first one way, then the other. 'It's an anomaly, isn't it? And I would guess, on the evidence so far found...'

'Evidence?' he asked drily.

'Clues, then. Do you know anything about its history?'

He shook his head.

She looked thoughtful. 'It has a whole mish-mash of styles, doesn't it?'

'Does it?' he asked ruefully. 'I'm afraid I wouldn't know. Have you done much reporting?'

'No, just some pieces about the countryside,' she said absently. 'Did you notice how the landing's been divided?'

'Divided?'

'Yes. Look at the coving. It stops.' Walking across to the end wall, she rapped her knuckles on it. 'I wonder if there's panelling underneath?'

'No,' he denied firmly. There was going to be enough disruption in the house without Phoenix

Langrish ripping down walls to look for panelling.

'The landing would originally have run along
to the end wall, as it does in the other direction.'
As though eager to be away from him, as though
on no account must she stand still, she opened a
bedroom door and walked inside to stare up at
the coving on that side. 'See how it starts again?
You could put this bedroom wall back where it
was originally, get the coving restored.'

'The bedroom would be smaller.'

'Yes, but worth it, I would have thou—'
Breaking off, she suddenly strode across to the
far wall and ripped a piece of loose paper free.

'Phoenix!' he exclaimed in mild exasperation.

Turning to look at him she said urgently, 'I
need to look in the loft space.'

'Why?'

'Because I think the house was built round an
older structure.'

'*Older?*' A small frown in his eyes, he asked,
'How old?'

'Medieval.'

'*Medieval*? Are you sure?'

'Not a hundred per cent, but look...'

Joining her, he stared at the small piece of
wood that just showed through where she'd torn
the paper. 'It's only an old beam,' he murmured

as she began picking away paper and plaster to reveal more of the wood.

'Yes, *old*,' she emphasised. 'And the majority of medieval houses *were* built of wood. Most have perished, of course. We can have the wood dated, but I'm confident that we'll find further evidence of it being medieval. Maybe an original Manor house,' she added excitedly. 'Probably fortified…'

'Whoa,' he cautioned. 'Let's not get carried away here…'

'But it is! I'm sure it is! Later occupants have built round it, and over the years it's been reinvented, if you like. Built on, added to—no *wonder* you didn't want to sell it.'

Yes, no wonder, he thought bemusedly.

'The loft?' she prompted.

'I don't know if it's safe…'

'But we have to look! You must want to *know*!'

Enthused by her urgency, he finally nodded. 'But just a *look*,' he cautioned. 'The entrance is through there. I'll go and get a torch. And don't go up without me!'

Walking out quickly, he ran lightly down the stairs, his mind buzzing with Phoenix's enthusiasm. Medieval? Did she really know what she was talking about? Or was enthusiasm and hope carrying her away?

Finding the torch in the kitchen, he'd turned to go back upstairs when there was an almighty crash followed by a yell of alarm.

CHAPTER TWO

'PHOENIX?' he called urgently. Racing up the stairs, he hurried into the first room, and stared in astonishment at the shattered window, the shards that lay on the bare boards, and at Phoenix, who was carefully removing pieces of glass from her jacket.

She gave him a small, rather shaken smile. 'Sorry, I didn't mean to yell. It rather took me by surprise.'

'Yes,' he agreed inadequately. 'Are you all right?'

'Oh, yes, not cut or anything—just gave me a fright.'

Still shocked, he glanced quickly through the broken pane, then carefully began edging the pieces of glass to one side with his foot. There was nothing to indicate what might have broken the window, and no one to be seen outside.

'Perhaps it was a bird,' she murmured. 'Crashed into the window and...'

'Yes,' he agreed thoughtfully. 'Or children. It's half-term, I believe, and an apparently empty house...' Remembering his own schooldays, and

34

the mischief he and his friends had got up to, it seemed a logical explanation, but he'd seen no children outside. 'I'll go and look.' He turned away, and she called him back.

'Torch?'

'What? Oh.' Handing it over, he ordered absently, 'Don't go up there without me.'

Returning down the rear staircase, he opened the back door and looked out. Nothing. No sign of anyone. Walking round to stand beneath the shattered window, he found no sign of a stunned bird, no sign of anything. He could hear the rooks in the trees at the far end of the field, a tractor somewhere, but nothing else. And if children had been throwing stones there would have been evidence of it on the landing.

Standing over at the old barn, where he'd parked his car, he walked slowly across to peer inside. Nothing.

Puzzled, eyes on the distant copse, he returned to the house. It might have been a bird—and then again it might not. But, whatever the cause, he would need to get a glazier out.

Grey eyes thoughtful, he walked back upstairs—and couldn't find Phoenix. Certainly she wasn't where he'd left her, although it didn't take a genius to figure out where she'd gone. Walking through to the front bedroom, he saw that the door that led to the loft was standing open. A pair of high-heeled shoes lay abandoned halfway up the narrow staircase.

Exasperated, he climbed up to find her balancing on a beam and staring up into the rafters.

'I told you to wait for me,' he stated mildly.

'Sorry,' she murmured absently as she continued to play the torch over the old beams above her.

'Find anything?'

'Yes. My God, Nash, they're nearly all intact!'

'The beams?'

'Yes. See how it's gabled at each end, with a fairly steep pitch? How the ridge purlin...'

'Pardon?'

'Oh, sorry, the long beam—see how it extends horizontally along the ridge from one end to the other?'

'Yes,' he agreed cautiously.

Turning, she smiled at him. 'It's one of the earliest and most simple designs. A tie beam roof, definitely medieval. It's beautiful,' she whispered. 'And so unexpected. To actually have survived... You could open up the landing ceiling...'

'No, no, no,' he reproved.

'But Nash! Think how it would look!'

'I am thinking. Of the mess, the draughts...'

'You have no soul.'

'I have a *practical* soul,' he argued. 'Do you need to take photographs?' Negotiating the beam behind her, he handed over the camera. 'Careful!' he warned urgently as she stepped back. 'You'll go through the ceiling!' Taking her notebook and the torch, so that she could have her hands free, he waited whilst she took several flash photographs of the roof.

'Come on, this floor doesn't look any too safe to me. We can argue about it when we're out of here.' Carefully backing up, steadying her as she did the same, he turned her in the doorway, and stilled. Forced close together in the narrow space, camera, notebook and torch between them, he stared down into her wide eyes.

'A moment waiting to happen,' he murmured, his voice soft, husky.

'No,' she whispered. She made a jerky movement, as though to flee, and he quickly prevented her.

'Yes.' Bending his head, he found her mouth with his, felt the tremor that ran through her. The tremor that ran through himself.

And he didn't want to stop.

He kissed her urgently, thoroughly, felt the same pleasure and pain he had felt ten years previously. A compulsion, a need, and as she shuddered, tried to push him away, he lost his balance.

Grabbing the doorframe to steady himself, he was thrown further off balance when she ducked under his arm and ran down the narrow stairway. Tripping on her abandoned shoes, she was forced to jump the last few steps.

By the time he joined her she was standing at the window, both arms hugged round her middle.

Quietly watching her, he knew that if he said the wrong thing now he would lose her.

Walking across, he put the torch and notebook down on the window seat. Standing behind her, he put gentle hands on her shoulders, and she flinched.

'Don't do this to me,' she begged.

'You can't ignore it.'

'Yes, I can.'

'But why?'

'Because it isn't what I want,' she insisted, sounding incredibly strained. 'And you can't expect me to...'

'I don't. I *don't*,' he repeated. 'It took me by surprise too, the feelings.'

'But it's absurd! It's been ten years, Nash!'

'I know.'

Slowly turning her, he stared down into her

beautiful anguished face. 'The moment you stepped from the car I knew. And so did you.'

'No.'

'Yes. Lie to me if you must, but don't lie to yourself,' he reproved gently.

'But I don't know you! I don't know that I ever did.'

'Then we'll take time to get to know each other.' Summoning every ounce of self-control, he encouraged, 'Tell me about the roof. *Is* it really medieval?'

'Yes, it...' Taking a deep, steadying breath, she stepped away from him. 'I've never seen one in such good condition. You must get those slates replaced. If we have any rain...'

'Yes.' Watching her, almost aching at her predicament, which surprised him, he added gently, 'Sit down and tell me what I have. Come on. You're the expert.'

She didn't move for a while, just continued to look troubled, and then she sat down and picked up her notebook. Opening it to a fresh page, she put on her glasses.

'And make it simple,' he ordered as he perched beside her.

She stiffened slightly, but when he made no move to touch her she allowed her shoulders to relax fractionally. Speaking quietly, she began to sketch, her movements jerky at first, but gradually smoothing out.

A wisp of hair was lying across her cheek, and he wanted to move it, tuck it behind her ear. A perfect ear, one he had once touched with his tongue. Maturity had firmed her features—maturity and knowledge. At eighteen her thoughts, opinions had been formed by others; now she had her own clever mind to formulate new ideas, to direct her life with intelligence and confidence, and he was finding it hard to come to terms with this ten-year jump. Then she had bombarded him with questions—How do you do this? How that? What's this for? That? Now she probably didn't need to. She had always been bright. Now she was brighter. He knew she'd got a first at Oxford, because he'd checked.

'And, of course, assuming it was once a Hall, a massive beam would have been thrown across the roof space, from wall plate to wall plate, to counteract the outward thrust on the walls.' Unaware of his inattention, pencil flying, she continued tensely, 'A central king post—or two queen posts, as you seem to have—and side struts were often supported on the tie beam to strengthen the structure. Further purlins—beams,' she hastily corrected, 'were set at intervals down the pitch like so, from apex to wall.'

Quickly adding more detail, her strokes sure and deft, to show him how it would have looked atop a medieval Hall, she continued, 'Rafters were inserted across at right angles, supported on the wall plate—the horizontal beam at wall level—at the bottom, and attached to the ridge purlin at the top. The wall plate itself was secured by stone corbels.

'Of course, by the fifteenth century there was less need for fortification and the structure would have been altered. Bedrooms and reception rooms would have been put in, the central hearth would probably have given way to wall fireplaces with roof chimneys, and, if the family was wealthy, stone would have been used round the outer walls. We might even find re-used medieval masonry. There would have been a huge courtyard—have you found any evidence of a courtyard?' she broke off to ask. Without looking at him.

Wrenching his attention back, he shook his head. 'But then, I haven't investigated that much.'

'Well, there would have been outbuildings, roof lines at various levels broken by tall chimney stacks...'

'Of which I still seem to have some.'

'Yes, so what we need to do now is check the

archives, census returns, ordnance survey maps, find out who owned it, who altered it—because by the seventeenth century it would have changed out of all recognition.'

'But it doesn't look seventeenth-century now. My aunt's solicitor described it as late eighteenth-century.'

'Yes, Georgian, because of course it changed again. The façade is definitely Georgian. So is the east wing.' Still busily sketching, she filled in the courtyard, added a few geese, and presented it to him. 'That's how it would have looked, I would guess, when it was first built. A fortified manor house with moat.' Jumping to her feet, she moved to stand a few paces away.

As though he hadn't noticed, he continued to stare at her sketch, then slowly smiled. 'I've seen one like that in, oh, I don't know—Herefordshire, I think.'

'Mmm, the Manor House at Lower Brockhampton, I expect.'

'And so it would be an awful pity to pull it down, wouldn't it?' he asked softly.

'Oh, yes, you mustn't do that.'

He looked up, and she looked hastily away. Removing her glasses, she began to chew on one of the stems.

'How long have you needed them?'

She gave an odd little jerk. 'What?'

'Your glasses. How long have you needed them?'

'Oh, not long. I only use them for close work. I'll go and do some research, I think, and then—'

'Really not interested?' he interrupted softly.

'Sorry?' she queried nervously.

'Already spoken for?'

She swallowed. 'Don't.'

'What are you so frightened of, Phoenix?'

'I don't know,' she said helplessly.

Leaning back, the sketchbook on his knee, he asked quietly, 'How much did I hurt you?'

'Unfair question,' she murmured evasively.

'Why?'

'Because...oh...' She sighed. 'Because I was eighteen, and at eighteen *everything* hurts.'

'I was trying *not* to hurt you,' he explained as he continued to watch her. 'I almost contacted you several times.'

'But common sense prevailed?' she asked, in a bitter little tone that puzzled him.

'Yes. I wasn't ready for a serious relationship. And it would have been serious, wouldn't it?'

'Would it? I really can't remember,' she retorted evasively as she went to collect her shoes.

She was lying. She hadn't forgotten it any more than he had. 'Then tell me how I go about restoring the Manor. It can't go back to what it was, can it?'

Pushing her feet into the high heels, she shook her head. 'Sadly, no. You could open it up to how it looked before the Regency period, or before the Victorians had a go at it. Restore some of those lovely cornices, expose some beams—but, no, you won't be able to get it back to how it was.'

'Pity.'

'Yes. And I'm not sure about the rules and regulations for altering a structure. You'd need a structural engineer—experts, anyway.'

'Stop babbling. I wonder what happened to the moat?'

'Filled in years ago, I expect.' Warily approaching him, she gathered up her bits and pieces and stepped back. 'There isn't much more I can do today, so I'll go and see what documentary evidence I can find.'

Getting to his feet, he stared at her for some moments in silence, and then he asked gently, 'Going to run for ever?'

She didn't answer, just turned and walked out.

Escorting her to her car, he fitted her wing mirror back on for her. 'It's only a temporary repair,' he warned.

'Yes,' she agreed. 'I'll call in to the garage.'

'And you'll come back tomorrow?'

Breathing shallow, tension in every line of her, she shook her head. 'I don't know. I don't *know*,' she emphasised agitatedly. 'Don't push me. Please don't do that.'

'All right.'

She gave a perfunctory smile that seemed aimed at the hedge, and climbed into her car.

Quietly closing the car door, he watched her reverse erratically out into the lane and drive away.

A cold shower? he wondered in grim amusement. Except he didn't have a shower. There was running water in the antiquated bathroom, but the bath looked as though it had been used for dipping sheep. And he wanted her. Couldn't believe how much he wanted her. Better start practising self-restraint, my friend.

Face showing nothing of his feelings, he returned inside. And if she didn't come back tomorrow he would go and find her.

He could understand her wariness—but her fear? What was it about him that frightened her so? A new experience for him, he thought wryly, to be unsure of something. Extremely patient when he needed to be, with women he had never needed to be. And that spoiled it. He didn't really know why women found him so attractive, unless it was his money, he thought cynically. Chrissie had said it was his watchful silences that females found intriguing. But then, Chrissie had said a lot of things.

Dismissing her, he ran lightly up to the top landing to begin a more thorough search for evidence of how the window had been broken.

He didn't find any stones. What he did find were several shotgun pellets embedded in the opposite wall. Picking them out, he tossed them thoughtfully in his palm. A shooting accident? It was the countryside, after all. With a rather disbelieving smile, he straightened, stared from the window, tried to determine the angle of the shots. The only two places remotely possible—the only places where someone wouldn't be seen—were the copse at the back of the house and the old barn. He thought it might be wise to have another word with the executor of his aunt's will. Find out exactly what *sort* of pressure had been put on his aunt to force her to sell.

For lack of anything else, he tore a strip of loose wallpaper off the wall and screwed the pellets into it, then put it in his pocket. He then went to clear up the broken glass. When he'd finished, he walked downstairs, locked up the house, and went round to retrieve his car from the barn. All four tyres had been slashed.

An expression in his grey eyes that very few people ever saw—and that those who did generally wished they hadn't—he walked the five hundred yards to the next property and asked to use their phone, having foolishly left his mobile at home in London.

Because of who he was, because he paid well, the garage that always serviced his car persuaded a local firm to send out a mechanic with four new tyres; the glazier arrived five minutes after. And five minutes after that the news was all round the village. Unasked, unannounced, they organised their own surveillance team. If someone was trying to deter their hero from restoring the Manor, they wanted to know who it was.

So did he.

Whilst car and window were being repaired, Nash walked to the copse, poked around for a few minutes, but didn't really expect to find anything. He didn't. He spent the rest of the waiting time idly looking for traces of the old moat. He didn't find that either.

After thanking the mechanic, and the glazier, he drove back to London.

Settling himself in his study, he picked up the phone and made several quick calls. One of them a repeat call to the private detective, another to make an appointment to see the executor of his aunt's will. He also rang the managing director of one of his companies, a company that dealt with home security. And, not only because he was the boss, but because he was liked and respected, someone would be at Oddly Manor within the next hour to find out what security arrangements were needed. Mouth pursed, feet hooked comfortably atop an old and battered desk, he smiled, because, suddenly, the boredom of the last few months was gone.

Glancing at his watch, he made a quick decision. He had a great many business interests apart from the five companies he owned outright, none of which couldn't be dealt with from the other end of a telephone line. He would take a holiday—for as long as it took. His secretary could always get in touch with him in an emergency on his mobile phone. A fact he informed her of when he rang her a few minutes later.

He also made a shopping list. He didn't dare have the electricity restored to the Manor until he'd had the wiring checked, so at the top of his list were storm lanterns, and then candles. He would need food, a camping stove, kettle, saucepan. Was there water downstairs? He would need to check.

Picking up the phone again, he rang his mother and told her to ring him on his mobile if she needed him. Not that she was particularly old, or infirm, but she sometimes needed him to talk to.

They chatted for a few minutes about the house; he asked after his stepfather, her health, what she'd been up to. Neither mentioned her stepson. Where *he* was concerned, no news was good news.

Half an hour later, whistling softly under his breath, he'd showered and changed, packed enough clothes for a week, found his old sleeping bag, and, on his way out, had a quiet word with the security guard who patrolled the building. He then went shopping, before driving over a hundred miles to see Miles Gordon, his aunt's solicitor and executor, to find out about intimidation. Because Phoenix had been right. He wasn't at all what he seemed.

It was late when he reached Oddly Manor, and he found one of the villagers waiting for him. Don Hopkins, he discovered, who owned a lock-up garage.

'Thought it might be best, Mr. Vallender. Heard what happened. I'll help you unload, shall I? Then I can take the car and lock it away safe. You want it, just ring, and I'll bring it round.'

'There's no need for that,' Nash denied quietly. 'I can easily walk down.'

'Easier this way,' he insisted, leaving no room

for argument. The villagers did things their way, and that was the way things would be done.

'Protecting your own?' Nash asked drily.

'Something like that. Not that you look as though you *need* protecting. Over six foot, are you?'

'Six two,' Nash confirmed with a faint smile.

'Thought so. These lanterns to go in?'

'Yes. How do you know *I* won't develop the land? I could be as profit-conscious as the developers.'

'But you aren't,' he denied, seemingly without a shred of doubt. 'Matthew Pinden still has keys, so we put you in a chair, bed and oil lamp. They'll do you for now.'

'Yes,' Nash agreed as he followed his new neighbour into one of the back rooms and surveyed the sparse creature comforts that had been provided.

'We cleaned the sink and toilet in the bathroom. Couldn't do much with the bath,' he added gloomily.

'No.'

'And you'll need an electrician,' he stated, before returning to the car.

'Yes,' Nash agreed again, with barely concealed amusement, as he hefted his box of groceries out of the boot. 'The village boasts one, does it?'

'Kurt Wengler. Send him round, shall I?'

'If he's not too busy.' Playing the game, he added, 'Perhaps you'd also let me have a list of what other services the village boasts. I shall eventually need carpenters, builders—'

'Roofers,' Don interrupted. 'Gardener. Old Lally Watkins used to work here, you know.'

'Did he?'

'Yes. Send him round, shall I?'

'Please.'

Don nodded, as though satisfied. 'Won't rip you off, we won't.'

'Good.' And the way he said it caused Don to look at him and grin.

Chuckling, Nash unloaded the last of his belongings and obediently handed over his car keys. Don gave him a slip of paper with his telephone number on it in return.

'Rev. Peters is looking out the history of the Manor for you,' he added laconically. Then, with a little salute, he climbed into the car, didn't, thankfully, over-rev the powerful engine, and drove away.

Still smiling, Nash walked inside and closed the door. Fit in or else, had been the silent message.

Walking into the sparsely furnished room, he laughed out loud. He'd thought he was taking charge of his own life. He'd obviously been wrong.

After unrolling his sleeping bag on the top of the bed, he lay down fully clothed. Ankles crossed, hands linked behind his head, he watched the shadows play over the high ceiling. And thought of Phoenix. Like a schoolboy, he thought with a wry smile. An aroused schoolboy. Because thoughts of her could do that. He had by no means been celibate over the past ten years, but none of the women he had known had made him feel like this. And it *wasn't* her looks that stirred him so. He didn't know what it was, only that it made him feel protective, and excited. He wanted to get to know her again. Wanted to kiss her again. But *not* balanced insecurely on one foot!

Softly, softly, catchee monkey. He was very good at softly, softly. Or always had been, he mentally qualified. He was inordinately glad that Chrissie was off the scene. Chrissie had been a mistake. She'd become greedy and demanding, and when he wouldn't play her games she'd left. To teach him a lesson, she'd said. How sad that the lesson he'd learned wasn't the one she wanted him to. He didn't like greed, or petulance, nor the fact that she'd thought him an easy option. As had a lot of other people, until they'd learned their mistake. It was a sad fact of life that most people seemed to want *something* from him. Chrissie had wanted a meal ticket. His aunt had wanted him to be brave. Developers wanted his land. What would Phoenix want? Just to investigate the Manor? He hoped not. She'd been nervous of him, evasive, but not—hating. And she'd been as aroused by him as he'd been by her. So there was hope. But ten years was a long time. People changed, *feelings* changed. And there had certainly been a lot of feelings, he thought with a small smile. One look across a crowded hotel foyer and he had wanted to see her again. Find out what she was like. Now he wanted to find out again.

With a soft sigh, he reached down to turn out the lamp. Dismissing Phoenix for the moment, he lay in darkness and used his considerable intelligence to work out several other things that were puzzling him.

Eyes closed, he drifted into sleep. And woke to the smell of burning.

CHAPTER THREE

COUGHING, eyes smarting, he stared at the flaming lamp, at the licks of flame that ran in an almost straight line for the doorway.

Cursing, he leapt to his feet, flung the sleeping bag over the lamp to smother the flames and hastily stamped out the small fires. If he'd taken his shoes off... He must have knocked over the lamp in his sleep. Or someone wanted him to think so. Beginning to think more clearly, he trod carefully back to the bed and found his torch. Switching it on, he removed the sleeping bag and stared at the lamp as it lay on its side, and then at the blackened floorboards where spilled oil had ignited. The door stood open. Had he left it that way? He couldn't remember.

Walking quietly out into the hall, he listened. He heard only the normal settlings of an old house, and then caught a faint, almost ghost-like breath of air on his cheek. Treading softly, he made his way to the old servants' quarters. Switching off the torch, he groped his way to the kitchen, felt a stronger draught and followed it to the old pantry. The window stood open. The window that wouldn't shut because it was warped. Phoenix had commented on it. And if he hadn't been such a light sleeper...

Returning to his room, he stared at the lamp. *Could* he have knocked it over? It was possible, he supposed. But he'd never been a restless sleeper, never, as far as he was aware, flung his arms around. He'd certainly never knocked anything else over in his sleep.

Walking across to the lamp, he slowly righted it, tested it for stability. The floorboards *were* uneven, but would a lamp, of its own volition, just fall over? Would expanding oil vapour ignite? Glancing at his watch, he saw that it was over two hours since he'd fallen asleep. Wouldn't the oil have cooled by now?

Returning to the hall, he proceeded to make a systematic search of the house. Every room, every cupboard. Nothing.

Returning to the pantry, he examined the open window, the windowsill, shone his torch out onto the ground below. Again, nothing. An accident, he told himself. Perhaps the lamp had been faulty.

The villagers had donated the lamp.

The villagers had a key.

Don't get paranoid.

With an amused smile, because his sense of

adventure *did* sometimes get the better of him, he returned to his room.

He spent the rest of the night dozing in the armchair, his feet on the bed, and as soon as it was light he cleared up all evidence of the fire, disguised the blackened boards with dirt from the fireplace, washed and shaved in the bottled water he'd brought with him, and waited for whatever else might happen.

At seven, a small, rather insignificant-looking man arrived. His private detective. About his own age, light brown hair, light brown eyes. He grinned at Nash, held out his hand.

'More mess?'

'More mess,' Nash agreed. 'What name are you using?'

'Dave Thomas. What am I?'

'Borough.'

'Borough?'

'Mmm.'

He laughed. 'A busybody from the Borough Council can cover a multitude of sins. What am I doing here?'

'Checking.'

'Checking,' he agreed, with rather devilish amusement on his puckish face. 'Who'll be here?'

'Builders, plumbers, electricians—you name

it, I'll probably have them. And—' hopefully
'—Miss Langrish, who's an expert on old
houses. She'll tell you about purlins and tie
beams. She's also very accident-prone. I don't
know what else she is. Don't know what *anybody*
else is. But I had a fire last night which might or
might not have been accidental. The tyres on my
car were slashed, a window was broken—with
these.' Handing over the pellets, he continued,
'And my aunt suffered similar "accidents" when
the developers were trying to force her to sell.'

'Mmm. I'll get someone to check out the developers and their employees. Does your left
hand know what your right's doing?' he asked
slyly.

'No,' Nash denied with amusement.

'And you're enjoying yourself enormously,
aren't you?'

'Yes.'

He nodded. 'I'll go check on—things.'

Kurt Wengler, electrician, presented himself at
eight o'clock sharp. Obviously a man of few
words. He nodded to Nash, walked in, and proceeded to tour the house. Nash let him get on
with it.

Lally Watkins and his grandson arrived soon
after—and they had too many words. Eager, ex-

cited, reminiscent, they dragged Nash all over the property, taking it in turns to tell him how it had been, what had been there, how they'd been keeping the place tidy for his aunt. When Nash could get a word in edgeways, he asked about a moat. Or a courtyard.

No, nothing like that, he was told. But him and his grandson could continue to keep the grounds in order if he liked. Nash liked.

Returning to the house, he saw the builder's van just drawing up. Didn't waste much time in this village, did they?

Going to meet him, he found he'd conveniently brought a carpenter with him, and gave them free access.

Leaving everyone to it, and with every confidence in Dave Thomas, he walked down to the café in the village for breakfast. When he returned, he discovered that the plumber had arrived, and had a mate. The electrician had an assistant, the builders had multiplied, and there was now a tarpaulin tied securely across the roof in the east wing.

Face showing only mild amusement, he began walking towards the barn, from where he'd decided he could keep an overall view of the proceedings, and then veered to his right when he heard voices from the back of the house. One of them belonged to Phoenix.

'Please, you mustn't touch it,' she pleaded.

'But he hasn't got any water,' the plumber argued lamely.

'Then he'll have to go without. I'm sure he won't mind.'

'He will mind,' Nash said mildly from behind her. 'And you have to decide,' he quietly informed the plumber, 'whether you are more afraid of offending me, or Miss Langrish.'

The plumber looked wary. As he should, Nash thought. 'He who pays the piper…'

'That's not fair!' Phoenix exclaimed.

'Yes, it is. And this particular payer needs water.'

'But nothing must be touched until it's been examined!'

'Until what's been examined? The water pipes? They aren't medieval, surely.' Cocking an eyebrow at her, he waited. She looked utterly delightful and he wanted to touch her, pull her into his arms.

'That's not the point!'

'Then what is?'

The plumber quietly returned to his plumbing.

Taking her arm, he steered her outside. She was dressed more appropriately today, in jeans and a navy sweatshirt, her hair piled up and held in place with what looked like a red bulldog clip. He smiled at her. 'I was beginning to think you weren't coming,' he said softly.

'I was doing some research,' she muttered. 'And you said you wouldn't let anyone touch anything until I'd examined it!'

'So I did.'

'And if you're going to put everything back to how it was then you can't have pipes here anyway!'

'But the pipes aren't medieval.'

'That is not the point! The house is back to *front*!'

'I'm sorry?' he queried in bewilderment.

'It's back to front!'

'What is?'

'The *house*! It's quite simple!' she exclaimed aggrievedly.

'Not to me.'

With an irritable sigh, she began crossly, 'The original frontage was here.'

'How do you know?'

'Well, look at it!' Swivelling round, she pointed. 'You can see the arch, for goodness' sake. You wouldn't have an arch like that at the back and not at the front!'

Frowning up at the arch clearly displayed in

the brickwork, he murmured, 'But surely neither would you have a doorway that tall...'

'Of course you wouldn't!' she said impatiently. 'Sorry, but I find it so frustrating when...'

'Fools?' he offered softly.

'Yes. Well, no, not fools, but when people won't understand the significance of it all! It's important, Nash!'

'Important to you,' he reproved quietly. 'Not everyone shares your love of history.'

'But it's part of our past! Our heritage! How can we learn if people keep pulling things down, building on top of them?'

'Not everyone does want to learn. Some people only look to the future. And you can't make them care just by the sheer force of your will.'

'I know, but...'

'But this is important to you, and a wretched plumber is *not* going to get in your way, is he?'

'But if you are going to restore it you won't want *pipes* there, will you?' she persisted doggedly. And not once had she made eye contact with him. But she'd obviously been doing a lot of thinking, making decisions, because her attitude today was vastly different from yesterday.

'Then where will I want them?' he asked gently. 'You don't know, do you? *Do* you?'

'No,' she muttered.

'And I really do need to have running water. Now, tell me why that arch is so high.'

'It isn't,' she denied gruffly. 'I mean, not originally. There would have been steps up to it leading into the Hall, the most important room in the house. Below that, on the level we're standing now, would have been the undercroft—used for storage of food and household necessities which would be needed in times of siege. You have to remember that these manor houses were fortified.' Back on her hobby horse, she continued enthusiastically, 'The walls were probably battlemented, with a parapet behind, and...'

Dragging her back to the point in hand, he asked firmly, 'So it was originally three storeys, not two?'

'Yes, the Hall itself would have been two storeys high, but open to the roof.'

Not wanting to get back on the subject of taking down his ceilings, he persevered. 'So the undercroft would have been below the Hall?'

'Yes. Windows were small for defensive reasons.'

'But the one upstairs...' He frowned.

'Was of a later design, when security wasn't so much needed.'

'And is that why the downstairs rooms have

such high ceilings? Because a whole *floor* was taken out?'

'No—well, yes, but the ceilings were put in later. And I know you can't go back to that—I *know* that—but if we could put the entrance back where it was…'

'Which would mean removing all the plumbing, the kitchen…'

'Well, yes, but…'

'But what?' he prompted gently. 'If I'm to sell it, or even live in it, I will need a kitchen.'

'You could put it in the east wing.'

'And then what?'

'Open up all these passageways, make it one large space again. An entry hall.'

'I already have an entry hall.'

'But it's on the wrong side!'

'Historically, yes. Practically, no. Which was no doubt why it was changed in the first place. Although I do agree about all those small passageways being opened up. Will you settle for a *large* kitchen, with plumbing, instead of an entry hall?'

'It isn't my house,' she said quietly, and, he thought, a little sadly.

'No,' he agreed. 'It isn't. Maybe I could have a little leaflet printed telling it how it was.'

'Maybe,' she agreed a trifle huffily. 'Do you still want me to carry on?'

'Yes, Miss Langrish, I want you to carry on. Didn't you sleep very well?'

Startled, she stared at him, and as quickly away. 'What?'

'Only I thought that maybe your aggression stemmed from tiredness.'

'I'm not aggressive,' she muttered.

'Just aware?'

'Don't.'

She'd barely taken a step towards the doorway, with him following, when there was an urgent shout from above—and a large piece of masonry crashed to the ground where they'd been standing.

He didn't consciously remember grabbing her to shelter her from flying debris, was only aware that he was holding her in a tight embrace, her head forced into his shoulder, and his own face turned away from lethal chips of stone. She was shaking. And he didn't want to move.

An old, remembered feeling—and one he had been trying to rediscover ever since, he admitted honestly. No one else had generated the warmth in him that she had, this feeling of—discovery. Yesterday's kiss had only confirmed that. His hands were against her back; her arms were round his waist. A reflex action against fear. And she was standing very, very still.

She lifted her head at the same moment he did, and they looked at each other.

'It *won't* go away,' he said gently. 'It will just get worse.'

She looked anguished for a moment, and he wondered why. Her glasses were askew, the bulldog clip dangling on a long piece of hair. Breathing agitated, she looked vulnerable and lost.

'Not hurt?' he asked gently as he righted her glasses.

'No,' she whispered. 'No,' she repeated more strongly as she stared at the shattered stone. 'Close,' she murmured shakily.

'Very.'

With a shuddery sigh, she undid the bulldog clip and twisted her hair back into its former position. Without looking at him again, she stepped inside the kitchen.

He watched her walk along the passageway, saw her trip on a pipe, saw the plumber put out a hand to save her. And then she was gone. And where was Dave Thomas when he needed him? A few yards away, he discovered when he looked round.

Dave nodded to him and disappeared round the side of the house.

The thunder of footsteps down the back stairway distracted his attention. The builder, a man in his early fifties, white-faced and shaking, breathing hard, erupted into the stone passageway. Blue eyes frightened, he stared at Nash, stared at the remains of the stone and shuddered. 'I tripped,' he stated thickly. 'Put out my hands to save myself, and the bloody stone just fell off. I'm sorry.'

'Not your fault,' Nash said easily.

'No, but... Can I have a word?' he asked seriously.

Nash nodded, led the way across to the barn.

'I've been a builder a long time,' he began quietly. 'Not a cowboy, but properly trained. Work's been slow of late, not much money around, and I won't say that building an estate here wouldn't have done me some good.'

'Because the developers offered you a contract if they managed to buy the land?' Nash prompted.

'Yes. But I like this village, like the people, and so I turned them down.' Blue eyes direct, he stared at Nash. 'Someone's been undermining the stonework. I know weathering, and I know wear and tear...'

'But parts of the building have been deliberately undermined?'

'Yes.'

'Helping with the decay. Helping it to fall down.'

'Yes.'

'Someone who knows what they're doing?'

'I would say so, yes.'

'And is it now too far gone to save?'

'Oh, no. God, no,' he said quickly. 'But I'm not an expert on ancient buildings,' he confessed, 'and if you're going to put it back as it was—whatever that is, because I didn't entirely understand what your Miss Langrish was talking about...'

'Not *my* Miss Langrish,' Nash denied quietly. Yet.

'Then you'd have to get proper experts in,' he concluded.

'But you can build, restore, put right?'

'Yes. What *are* you going to do with it?'

Nash smiled again. 'I don't know,' he confessed. 'Any ideas will be gratefully received.'

'Well, I'd repair the roof of the east wing for a start. Should never have gone like that. Whoever put it up wants shooting.'

'I'm informed by Miss Langrish—reliably, I'm sure—that it was put up in the late eighteenth century, when, one assumes, perhaps erroneously, builders were—um—professionals.'

'That one wasn't,' he stated dismissively.

'And then what?'

'Make good.'

'What about interior structure? Can that be altered?'

'Depends what you want.'

'I don't *know* what I want. All those passageways at the back opened up, perhaps. And Miss Langrish seems to think that the landing was open at one time, although I have no desire to lose *all* the bedrooms.'

'Then why don't we walk round it, and you can tell me what you might want, and I'll tell you what I think?'

'Sounds sensible.'

'You could apply to have it listed. I've been looking into it. If there's a building you think should be preserved because it's of special architectural or historic interest, you can ask the local council's planning department to serve a building preservation notice. If they grant it, it will protect the building for six months. It's a bit complicated, because notice has then to go to the Secretary of State for the Environment and he can decide yes or no. But if they agree to list it, it might mean you can't alter it.'

'Ah.' All of this Nash knew, but he often found it enlightening to listen to other people's opinions.

'But if it falls down anyway...' he began pointedly.

'Mmm,' Nash agreed.

'And,' he continued, 'you'll need planning permission if you're intending to demolish anything, alter anything structural. I'd get yourself an architect.'

'I already have one. Was there anyone with you on the roof?' Nash asked casually as they began to walk back to the house.

'With me? Oh, I see what you mean. Could have been any one of us who tripped.'

It wasn't what he'd meant, but he let it lie.

'Matt and Ernie were with me. Only youngsters, but good boys all the same. And Miss Langrish had been up there earlier, just standing on the walkway looking down at the back.'

Not commenting on that, Nash asked, 'And what was it you tripped over?'

Halting, the builder looked thoughtful for a moment. 'Don't know. I was in such a panic that I might have killed someone, I didn't stop to look.'

Continuing on to the house in silence, Nash

finally asked, 'Will you keep what you told me to yourself?'

'About the undermining?'

'Yes.'

He nodded. 'What will you do?'

'I don't know.' At the moment, he added to himself.

'Water's on,' the plumber told him warily as they walked in. 'Only cold, though.'

'Fine.'

Gaining confidence, he added, 'Water heater's knackered.'

'Thank you,' Nash said drily. 'Let me know what I need, what it will cost, how long it will take.'

'Yes, sir.'

By the end of the day he had electricity in some rooms, water, and a headache. The house needed rewiring, replumbing, repointing. A great deal of plaster was now missing from the landing and the end bedroom, where Phoenix had discovered the beam. And just where *was* Phoenix? He'd allowed her to avoid him for most of the day, but now he wanted to see her. Her car was still outside so she must be here somewhere. Everyone else had gone bar Dave Thomas. He didn't know where he was either.

He found them both in the loft. Perched on rafters, they were chatting away like old friends—or, rather, Phoenix was chatting, the way she'd once used to chat to him. Dave was looking fascinated. She no longer wore her glasses.

A bare lightbulb on a cable was dangling over one of the rafters. With no better ideas in mind, he joined them.

Dave nodded respectfully and got to his feet. Phoenix looked away.

'I have some more checking to do,' Dave said. 'Nice talking to you, Miss Langrish.' Passing Nash, he winked, and clambered down to the room below.

'What's wrong?' Nash asked her softly.

'Nothing,' she denied.

'Good, because I need your help.'

'What sort of help?'

'Restoration help. Hungry?'

Turning to look at him, she asked defiantly, 'Why?'

'Because I thought we might walk down to the pub and have something to eat.' Holding out his hand, he waited, then let it drop to his side as she scrambled unaided to her feet.

'Marson...'

'Who?'

'The builder. He wasn't very complimentary about Georgian workmen. We need to re-roof the east wing.'

'We?' she queried pointedly.

He smiled. 'Mind the step,' he said absently, then caught her as she tripped anyway. Catching her hand, refusing to let it go, he pulled her down to the ground floor. Leading her out into the sunshine, he tugged her through the gate and began walking along the lane in the opposite direction to the village.

'Probably pay for this,' he murmured conversationally.

'Pay for what?'

'The unusually good weather.'

'Oh.'

'Unbend, Phoenix; I'm not your enemy. Tell me what else we need to do.'

After an obvious struggle with whatever grievances were troubling her, she murmured, 'I think he's right.'

'Good. Outside or inside?'

'Sorry?'

'Do you wish to sit inside or outside?' he repeated patiently.

'Oh, outside, please.'

'What will you have to drink?'

'A glass of lemonade will be fine, thank you.'

'Sure?'

'Yes.'

He nodded, seated her at a table, smiled vaguely at the other two people sitting outside and went inside to get the drinks and a menu.

Carrying a pint for himself and her lemonade, he placed the menu before her. 'The waitress will be out in a minute to take our order.' Acting on impulse, he added quietly, 'I had a fire last night.'

Looking away, she stared at the other people in the garden. 'You weren't hurt?'

'No.'

'And no damage was done to the house?'

'Nothing worth mentioning.'

'Then why are you telling me?'

'Because I think someone started it,' he explained simply.

She looked back. 'Me?'

He shook his head. 'All four tyres on my car were also slashed.'

'And a window was broken.'

'Yes.'

'What else?'

'Slates going missing from the roof. Lead. A number of small incidents that aren't quite explainable.'

'But no one's been hurt?'

'No, but you're very accident-prone, aren't you? So be careful.'

She looked down. 'Who's Mr Thomas?' she asked as she peered myopically at the menu, clearly unable to read a word of it.

Taking it out of her hand, he murmured with hidden amusement, 'Borough.'

'Borough?'

'Mmm, something to do with safety regulations,' he added with sudden inspiration. 'And you can have a ploughman's, chicken curry, jacket potato or a selection of sandwiches.'

'Ploughman's,' she murmured. Finally looking up, she stared at him. 'I'm wasting my time, aren't I?'

'No,' he denied gently. 'And I did ask Lally Watkins senior about a moat and courtyard. He didn't have any knowledge of either.'

'It was a long time ago.'

'He *is* a long time ago!' he retorted humorously. 'He's eighty if he's a day.' Sipping his pint, he watched her. 'I *am* interested, Phoenix, but I have to be practical.'

'I know. I'm only supposed to identify things, and then leave it up to the owner to make decisions.'

'Mmm,' he agreed with a smile. 'Galling, ain't it?'

She didn't smile back.

'But I still need your help. Marson doesn't know anything about history; neither do I. Mike—the architect,' he promoted, in case she didn't remember who Mike was, 'will need instruction. We'll *all* need your help in deciding what to do for the best. So stop sulking and help me.'

With a little sigh, she stared off to one side. 'I think you ought to talk to Professor Morton. I don't really want anything to eat.' Getting abruptly to her feet, she hurried away, and he watched her, eyes thoughtful.

A troubled lady. Sad and hurting. Because of him. He remembered the infectious laugh she had given when she'd first arrived. Before she had seen him. And he wanted the laughter back.

CHAPTER FOUR

As soon as she was out of sight he left his pint and took a diagonal route through the sparse woodland opposite the pub, to cut out the bend in the lane. Easily outpacing her, he waited beneath a large tree. Unaware of being watched, her face sad, she yelped in alarm when he reached out and pulled her gently into the shadows.

Arousal was swift as he backed her against the tree. The feel of her against him, even as stiff as she was, as she tried to hold herself away, undermined every other thought.

'Running won't solve it, Phoenix,' he murmured huskily.

'You nearly gave me a heart attack, grabbing me like that,' she protested raggedly. 'And you lied to me.'

'Don't evade the issue,' he reproved gently as he took in every detail there was to take. The tousled hair, the perfect cheekbones, and a mouth to tempt the strongest man.

Breathing agitated, she frantically shook her head. 'I'm not. You did lie. Dave Thomas is no

more from the Borough than I am. And I don't
want this! I *don't*!'

'Yes, you do—and no,' he agreed, 'Dave
Thomas is not from the Borough. He's a private
detective.'

'Investigating me?' she asked stiffly.

'No, the developers who want the land.'
Removing her bulldog clasp, he clipped it to his
shirtsleeve, and as she stiffened, tried to pull
away, he threaded his hands through her lovely
hair so that his wrists framed her chin.

'Look at me.'

She glanced defiantly up.

'Why does the thought of being intimate with
me frighten you so much? You used to smother
me with kisses…'

'Don't,' she pleaded.

'Why? I want to hold you, touch you. I want
all these ridiculous preliminaries over with. And
they are ridiculous. We both know what we want,
what our bodies want. We both feel as we felt
ten years ago. Why pretend? You make my heart
ache, Phoenix.'

Staring at his throat, she whispered huskily,
'And you think I should fall into your arms as
though those years never existed?'

'Yes. *Yes*,' he repeated huskily. 'Now
kiss me.'

Her lower lip trembled, and it was too much.

Gathering her against him, he kissed her, and she jerked as though she'd been shot. But she wanted it as much as he did. Her hands gripped his shirt tighter, and with a little groan she kissed him back. And passion ignited as it had all those years before. If he hadn't been sharing a flat, if she hadn't lived with her parents, if she hadn't been just eighteen years old, they would have consummated that passion then. And perhaps the violent exchange now would have been muted. Perhaps.

He could feel the heat of her, the desire as she kissed him back with an urgency that almost made his feelings spiral out of control. Pushing his hands up beneath her sweatshirt, he revelled in the warmth of her flesh, unhooked her bra to free her breasts to his urgent touch. She gasped, moved her mouth to his neck and grasped him tighter.

Holding her as tight, he tried to regulate his breathing.

'Don't rush me,' she breathed agitatedly. 'I don't want to make love to you in the woods.'

'Don't you?' he asked thickly.

'No—oh, God, someone's coming.'

Hearing the distinct sound of a tractor trundling down the lane, he pulled her quickly round behind the tree.

'I was so determined this wouldn't happen,' she said shakily. '*So* determined. I told myself and told myself all last night that it wouldn't. Because I don't want this. I don't.'

'Logic and desire aren't on the same list, Phoenix,' he pointed out gently.

'I know that. I *know*. My mind says one thing, my body another, and I hate you for it. I hate you,' she said feebly. Putting up a shaky hand to touch his mouth, she stared at what she was doing. 'You spoilt everything, Nash,' she said quietly. 'Did you know that? Every man I met was measured against you. Found wanting against you.' Looking up, she stared into his eyes. 'I have never wanted anything as I wanted you. Ten years is a long time to remember passion. When I saw you standing behind my car yesterday, I wanted to run away.'

'I know.'

'*Should* have run away.'

'It wouldn't have helped.' The warmth of her body against his, the feel of her fingers against his mouth as he spoke sent a new thrill of desire through him.

'I don't know what I said. I have no memory of it—only of what I felt. I walked round the house seeing nothing, because an eighteen-year-old's hurt is remembered. A first love affair is remembered. And I *was* in love with you. The most exciting thing to ever happen to me. The most amazing, frightening, turbulent thing. I ate, drank, slept you. You were all I could think about, talk about, and the moments away from you were—agonising. You see? I remember it still. In the three short weeks that we knew each other, you changed my life for ever. And when you went to see your friend off yesterday I stood at the back of the house and shook, clutched the stone walls for support and shook. Yes, I want you,' she added in a whisper as her eyes returned to his mouth. 'I have never stopped wanting you, but...'

'But where will it end? Where will it lead? I don't know.'

'And I don't know if I can trust you,' she added. 'If something else should come along, something more important...'

'I was twenty-five, Phoenix,' he argued gently. 'Little more than a boy. I wanted so many things. When the chance came to work in the States...'

'You didn't hesitate.'

'Oh, I did, Phoenix. I didn't want to leave you.'

'But the promise of money and common sense prevailed,' she retorted bitterly.

'Yes,' he admitted honestly, 'because I eventually came to the conclusion that it wouldn't work. If I hadn't gone, I might have begun to resent it. Alternatively, if you had come with me, not gone up to university, you might have come to resent me. If I could have met you now for the first time...'

She gave a sad smile, moved her fingers to trace his cheekbone. 'Always so practical. Always so honest. Logic must always outweigh emotion. You aren't even ashamed, are you?'

'Ashamed?' he asked in surprise. 'No. Regretful, maybe, that I didn't handle things differently.'

'But you didn't want to see me again. Why? If, as you said, the passion was real, why didn't you get in touch when I'd finished my degree?'

'I don't know. And anything I say now will sound like excuses. Maybe they are excuses. A hungry young man wanting to make his mark on the world. I think I eventually persuaded myself that the feelings weren't real. That there would be other women with equal power. And perhaps, too, I didn't want my illusions of you shattered. If you had changed—university *does* change people. But when I saw the article about you...'

'It seemed like fate?' she mocked.

'Mmm.'

'I'm not the person I was, Nash. No longer so idealistic, no longer so naive. I grew up.'

'I know.'

'Perhaps we need to get it out of our system. Perhaps that's all it is.'

'Perhaps.' But he didn't believe it any more than he thought she did.

Her stomach gave an embarrassing rumble, and his smile quirked attractively. 'Ready for that meal now?'

She gave an odd, rather sad smile. 'Practical Nash. Can you do me up?' she asked awkwardly.

He kissed her nose. Turning her round, he lifted her sweatshirt, manfully resisted the near-overwhelming urge to touch her breasts again, settled her bra in place and hooked it closed. Tugging down her sweatshirt, he put his arms round her and kissed her neck through her hair. And it was hard to pretend a normality he didn't feel. But he would dearly love to know what was really troubling her.

As they walked back to the pub she rescued her clip from his sleeve and twisted her hair back into place.

She was as tense as he was.

Leading her inside, and into a dark corner, he

bought fresh drinks, ordered their meal, and returned to sit beside her. Shoulder to shoulder, thigh to thigh. She played distractedly with a beer mat.

There were a few others in the pub—an elderly couple, some youngsters at the far end—but no one near enough to disturb them. Eyes on her profile, forearms resting on the edge of the table, he said quietly, 'I want you.' And the mat she was holding cracked in half. Taking it from her, he held one of her restless hands in his. 'The moment you stepped from the car yesterday, I wanted you.' Lifting her hand, he touched her fingers to his mouth. 'I want to be with you. Hold you, love you, talk with you, laugh. Stay with me tonight.'

Her breathing arrested, then hiccuped into life, and her free hand curled convulsively on the table.

'Let me do all the things I didn't do ten years ago.'

The waitress interrupted them with their order, and the look Nash gave her made her heart race.

She gave a shaky smile, and fled.

Releasing Phoenix's hand, he put her meal before her, handed her her knife and fork, and stared at his lasagne with a wry smile. Picking up his own fork, he began to eat, watched

Phoenix from the corner of his eye as she picked at her meal.

'Frightened?' he asked softly, and her mouth twisted into a self-mocking grin.

'Terrified.'

'But resigned to your fate?'

She gave a funny little sigh, and put down her fork. 'I don't think I can eat this.'

'Neither can I.' Abandoning his half-eaten meal, he got to his feet. 'I need to make a phone call. And I've left the mobile at the Manor. Don't go away.'

He asked the bartender for the phone, and was directed into a side passage. Taking some change from his pocket, he rang Don Hopkins and asked him to bring his car to the pub. He then spent a few minutes looking through the local directory before making another quick call.

Returning to the bar, he saw that Phoenix had also abandoned her meal and was staring rather helplessly into her drink. He had known women with classical beauty that men raved about, known women with voluptuous curves, but he had never known a woman who made him feel as Phoenix made him feel. There was a vulnerability about her, and sometimes a wicked flicker of danger in those lovely eyes. A hauntingly sweet face, sensuous and appealing. A clever mind, and a delicate and slender body that made him feel protective—and extraordinarily aroused.

As though aware of being watched, she suddenly looked up, held his eyes for long, long moments, and he wanted the world to disappear. Didn't want the mundane process of driving to a hotel, checking in. Waiting. But the Manor was uninhabitable, so there was little choice, and he was experienced enough to make the transition as painless as possible.

Walking across, unaware that the waitress watched him with hungry eyes, that the barman watched Phoenix, he rejoined her, gave her a rueful smile. 'Five minutes.'

She didn't ask what was five minutes, just nodded, then gave a rueful smile of her own. 'I don't have a toothbrush.'

'I'll get you one.'

'I'm trying to sound brazen and blasé, but I feel sick.'

'Nerves.'

'I know.'

'They'll pass.'

'I know that, too.'

'Because…'

She looked at him, and he sensibly kept quiet. He had no right to ask about past loves. But the thought of other men who might have touched her made him feel ill.

Seeing his car pull up, he excused himself again. 'Finish your drink. I won't be a moment.'

He walked out to meet Don, and took the car keys he handed over. 'Do you need a lift home?'

Don shook his head. 'Let me know when you'll be back.'

'In the morning, I expect. Could you call into the Manor and tell Mr Thomas? Ask him to lock up?'

'Will do,' he agreed laconically.

'What do you drink?'

Don grinned. 'Malt whisky. A good one, mind.'

Nash nodded, waited until Don was out of sight, then returned to collect Phoenix.

He found the hotel without difficulty.

'It looks very opulent,' she murmured as they walked across the gravel courtyard.

'Mmm.'

'How did you know it was here?'

'Looked it up in the pub and then rang to make a reservation.'

'We don't have any luggage.'

He smiled. 'Already explained. We drove up from London to see Oxford, and found ourselves too tired to drive back.'

He registered with the minimum of fuss, collected the parcel they had for him, and escorted Phoenix up to their room.

'Tea and sandwiches will be brought up shortly.'

'Thank you. What's in the parcel?'

'New underwear for both of us, toothbrushes, razor, comb. I asked the manager to send someone out for—necessities.'

'Very efficient.'

'I didn't want you to have to go to the bother of washing out your knickers in the basin,' he explained blandly.

She bit her lip. 'So thoughtful.'

'Mmm.' Opening the door for her, he ushered her inside.

A large double bed dominated the *en suite* room, flanked by a dressing table, wardrobe, and two armchairs. Tossing the parcel onto the bed, he watched her wander round touching things before opening the door to the bathroom and peering inside. 'I'll have a shower,' she said quietly. Without waiting for him to answer, she went inside and closed the door. She also locked it.

Taking the tray the waiter brought, he put it on the dressing table, then lay on the bed and turned on the television. He looked extraordinarily calm. He wasn't. He felt as restless as a young boy about to take his first exam. He tried to think of anything except the fact that a few yards away Phoenix was naked. And wet.

He heard the shower go off, and lazily turned his head as the bathroom door opened. Hair piled on top of her head, damp wisps escaping, she was wearing one of the hotel's towelling robes that he had asked them to provide.

'Tea and sandwiches are on the dressing table,' he said quietly as he rolled to his feet. Scooping up the parcel, he walked into the bathroom.

After showering and shaving, managing *not* to cut himself when he found to his chagrin that his hand was shaking, he cleaned his teeth and put on the other robe before returning to the bedroom. Phoenix was perched on the edge of the bed, facing the television and nibbling a sandwich. Her back looked extremely tense.

Walking up beside her, he put a gentle hand on the back of her neck. Taking the sandwich from her, he put it back on the plate and perched beside her. 'You can change your mind,' he murmured gently. 'Go home, do anything you choose. It isn't compulsory. Or we can talk, get to know each other. The choices are all yours.'

'I don't want to go home,' she denied in a

husky little voice that made his heart race. 'I want you.'

'I know.'

'I've been sitting here shaking, and telling myself that I'm a fool, but I want you. I quite hate myself for that.'

'I know that too.'

Turning her head, she looked into his face. 'Do you?'

'Yes.'

Voice a bare whisper, she said, 'I need to clean my teeth.'

'Toothbrush is in the mug. The pink one.' He smiled.

She nodded and hurried away.

Whilst she was cleaning her teeth he put the cover back over the sandwiches, put the napkin over the teapot, reseated the bottle of wine in its ice bucket and transferred the tray to the bedside table just as Phoenix came out of the bathroom. She'd removed the clip and her hair hung loose over one shoulder.

He smiled at her and held out his hand.

She took a funny little breath and walked into his arms. Burrowing her face into his neck, she slid her arms round him. He didn't rush her, just gently rubbed her back as he felt her trying to regulate her breathing.

'It's all right to gasp,' he said softly, and she looked up to smile. And then her smile died.

'Nash…'

'Shh.' Transferring his hand to the nape of her neck, he bent his head to kiss her—and felt the leap their bodies made. With a groan, he scooped her up and laid her on the bed. Rolling to cover her, he forced his hands into her thick hair and began to kiss her as he had wanted to kiss her for the last twenty-four hours. Arousal was swift and aching, and he didn't think a slow progression would be possible. Knew it wouldn't as her restless fingers found the opening in his robe and parted it, parted her own until her naked breasts touched against his chest and his thigh found the opening between hers.

Breathing erratic, kisses frantic, compulsive, deep and hungry, he wrenched both robes aside so that flesh could touch flesh from shoulder to ankle. He hated using protection, but he wasn't a fool. He hadn't seen her for ten years, nor she him, and so, for both their sakes, he took a moment to protect them both before finally finding the release they had been denied ten years before.

Her fingers still biting into his buttocks, her ankles gripping his thighs, he rested his face against her neck and closed his eyes. Both were breathing erratically, and it seemed to take a very long time to come down from such an impossible height. It hadn't only been a release from tension, or frustration, nor had it been only sexual, but something more. Something he didn't know how to define. He only knew that he had never felt like this in his life before.

As she eased her legs down, released her frantic grip, he lifted his head and stared down into her face. Gazed deep into her eyes, and then gently kissed her again. His heart was slamming slowly into his ribcage, hers was fluttering like a little lost bird, but the sensuality of her kiss would remain with him for a very long time. Long fingers stroked his back, her toes scraped gently against his shin, and her body was warm and soft and pliable, and he wanted to touch every inch of it with his mouth, his tongue.

Still tense, still wanting, his flesh hot, he freed her mouth, ran his tongue across her lower lip. 'Worth waiting for?' he asked thickly.

'Yes.'

'I'll be back in a moment.'

Releasing her swiftly, he padded into the bathroom to dispose of the protection, and returned in seconds. She lay as he had left her, eyes open, her body as tense as his.

Tossing the small towel he was carrying onto the bed, he removed his robe and knelt above her. One knee at either side of her long legs, he held her eyes with his and helped her take her arms out of her own robe.

'I need you naked.'

Her voice as soft and husky as his, she whispered, 'I am naked.'

'And so exquisitely beautiful.'

'A person,' she chided.

'Yes. Smile,' he ordered.

'Not possible.'

Her eyes looked almost black as she reached for his thighs, and he drew in a swift breath. 'Not fair.'

'Necessary,' she countered.

'I feel…'

'Yes.'

Moving downwards, he put one hand to either side of her, slowly lowered his weight, and began to kiss her nose, her mouth, chin, her neck, felt the shiver she gave as he reached her full breasts, spent an inordinately long time examining them with his tongue whilst she gently scraped her fingernails along his spine, and then not so gently as he reached her hastily contracted stomach. Knees poised on the end of the bed as he continued to shuffle backwards, he felt the most unbelievable warmth fill him as he reached the most secret part of her, and her gasp only added to his warmth.

He kissed her inner thighs, her knees, and finally, kneeling on the floor, her toes and the high arch of her dainty feet.

And then he began all over again.

He allowed her to make her own exploration until they were both limp and exhausted.

'I feel a hundred and four,' she said shakily as he returned to lie beside her, and even then they had to touch.

'Two hundred and three.'

She gave a little snort of laughter that sounded oddly nervous, and rolled to face him. Reaching behind her, she tugged the edge of the quilt across her hips.

He moved it back. 'Not allowed,' he said softly.

'Isn't it?'

'No.' Putting his warm palm where the quilt had been, he began to stroke her hip gently. She shivered. 'I have this overwhelming need to keep touching you.'

Eyes locked on his, she whispered helplessly, 'Oh, Nash.'

He gave a crooked smile, eased her more warmly against him.

'Did you expect that after we'd made love the hunger would go away?' she asked quietly.

'I don't know. I don't think very clearly when you're near me.'

'I can't think at all!'

'Good.'

They didn't smile at each other, just examined expressions. 'Hungry?' he asked quietly.

'Starving.'

'I don't suppose the sandwiches will be too badly curled. Or I can send down for a meal.'

She shook her head. Releasing him with a shy little gesture that delighted him, she scrambled upright. Stacking the pillows behind her, she reached across him to remove the cover from the sandwiches, and took one.

'Women like you, don't they?' she asked.

Tilting his head back so that he could see her face, he said softly, 'Do they?'

'Yes. You're extraordinarily sexy—but I don't know why,' she murmured with a little frown. Finishing one sandwich, she reached for another. 'I mean, you're fantastically attractive, and your eyes are to die for, but you don't look—dynamic. And you are. Effortlessly clever, you hide your skills behind sleepy grey eyes. And that's dangerous. Very, very dangerous.'

He merely smiled and returned his head to its former position.

'You don't boast, or show off, no ostentatious signs of your vast wealth, and so I don't quite know what it is that makes you so head-turningly attractive. But people somehow know you're different; they just don't know why.'

'How do you know I have vast wealth?' he asked softly as he began idly to draw circles on her knee with his fingertips. 'And don't eat all the sandwiches.'

When she didn't immediately answer, he tilted his head again. She'd gone pink. 'Mmm?'

'I—rang someone about you.'

'Who?'

'The editor of one of the national dailies. He's a friend of mine.'

'Ah.'

'He said you were frighteningly clever, disgustingly rich, and that you weren't what you seemed. But then, I knew that.'

'Yes. *When* did you ring him?'

'Last night.'

'And that's why you were intimidated this morning?' he mocked gently.

'I was not intimidated. But *suspecting* you had probably made your mark on the world was one thing. *Knowing* you had...'

'Made you wary?'

'Made me feel, *momentarily*,' she emphasised, 'out of my league.'

'But not any more?'

'No. When I first knew you I was probably quite overwhelmed by you, because despite you saying you were little more than a boy you didn't *seem* like a boy. You seemed worldly and experienced, and I think that memory of my younger self keeps coming into what's happening now.' With a funny, self-mocking little smile, she added, 'I want to appear experienced and insouciant, but the truth of the matter is, I don't feel either. I feel lost and adrift, as though none of this is happening—and I don't want to be afraid that you'll find me immature.'

'I find you delightful,' he said seriously.

'Yes, but you don't know me, do you? Any more than I know you.'

'Something that's easily remedied.'

'Yes,' she agreed, almost doubtfully. 'I hope I like you.'

He chuckled and hoisted himself up to sit beside her. Filching one of her pillows, he kissed her nose. 'I hope so too.' He also hoped she wasn't about to ask for reassurances—reassurances he couldn't yet give. He wanted to know her, and he wanted to make love to her, and that, for the moment, was enough.

Reaching for a sandwich, he popped the small triangle into his mouth. Balancing the plate on her thighs, he began to open the wine.

'No champagne?' she asked in tones of severe disappointment.

'Don't like it.'

'And so I don't get it?'

'Correct.' Pouring it out into their glasses, he handed her one and gave a silent toast, his eyes amused.

'Why are you laughing?'

'Because impersonal hotel rooms are a new experience for me. I should have taken you to Paris.'

'Too long to wait,' she said softly.

'Yes.' And he wanted her again. Felt such overwhelming desire for this slim, beautiful girl that his wine spilt over the edge of his glass and dripped onto his chest.

Her eyes followed the movement and she gave a little shudder. 'Oh, God,' she whispered. 'I want...'.

'Then do it,' he ordered thickly.

Hand shaking, she removed the plate of sandwiches, placed her glass on the bedside table, twisted herself round and began to lick the wine from his chest. His body felt as though it had gone into spasm. *She'd* wanted to appear insouciant? he thought in amazement. He'd never felt like this in his life! For such a slender, innocent-looking girl to be able to play him like a violin was even more amazing. How many lovers had she *had*? he wondered with a spurt of savage jealousy that was as foreign to his nature as blackmail. Then all thoughts were suspended, and only feelings mattered.

A long, long time later, they lay twined exhaustedly together, and even then they continued to stroke each other. The remainder of the sandwiches lay abandoned on the floor; the wine bottle was empty. An evening of sensuous pleasure, he thought sleepily as she snuggled against him like a kitten. He didn't know what she was thinking, only how she felt. How he felt.

He woke in the night to find her watching him, leaning up on her forearms, hair hanging over one naked shoulder. Her eyes were fixed on his face, and his body changed again. He didn't ever remember being so consistently aroused.

'I was kissing you,' she said simply.

Reaching out, he tangled his fingers in her hair. 'Why?'

'Because I need the practice?'

'Don't be flippant, and you don't need the practice.'

'No,' she agreed soberly. 'With you, I... Even in sleep I want you.'

Not what she had been going to say, but he let it lie. 'Don't hate me,' he said quietly.

She lowered her lashes. 'I don't. But I can't behave naturally with you. I don't know what to say to you, how to behave.'

'Because we don't know how we feel about each other,' he agreed. 'Only how our bodies feel, our senses.'

'Yes.'

'But if we explore our senses, perhaps we'll find the people inside. Kiss me,' he ordered huskily.

Leaning forward, eyes still lowered, she rubbed her lips against his, and as her breasts brushed his chest he slid his other arm round her waist and eased her to lie on top of him. He didn't enter her; he didn't need to.

They fell asleep again, wrapped in each other's arms, and when he woke she was still curled against him. Long lashes dark on her cheeks, hair tumbled, lower lip pouting, like a child. Such a sensuous little thing, he thought as he gently moved her hair away from her face. And felt a rather overwhelming regret that he hadn't been her first lover. That he hadn't been the one to teach her.

She opened her eyes, and he felt his heart ache. Such big eyes, brown and dark and mysterious.

'What time is it?' she whispered.

Glancing at the clock, he told her, 'Eight.'

'I have an appointment with the archivist at ten.'

'Cancel it.'

'I can't,' she said regretfully. 'He's taking so much trouble for me.'

'I imagine most men would go to a lot of trouble for you.'

'Do you?'

'Yes.'

Touching her fingers to his face, she said quietly, and perhaps a little sadly, 'I'm not promiscuous, Nash. I've never behaved with anyone else as I've behaved with you.'

'Good.'

'Have you?'

'No.' And it was true. He hadn't. Not like this. 'I don't want to move.'

'Neither do I, but I must.'

'Then we'd better get up.'

'Yes.'

'Don't kiss me,' he warned.

'No.'

They continued to stare at each other, and then she sighed. 'I'll go and have my shower.'

'I'll join you.'

'Order breakfast first.'

'Mmm.'

Rolling free, she padded into the bathroom. This time she didn't lock the door. But she'd been thinking in the night, hadn't she? Rationalising. And he didn't want her to do that.

Quickly ordering breakfast to be left outside their room, he joined her.

When they were eventually ready, he drove her back to Mincott Oddly. Leaving the car with Don, they walked along the lane towards the Manor.

'An unsatisfying ending to a satisfying night,' he said softly. 'A suspension of rational thought would make things easier.'

'For you? Or me?'

'You.'

'No, it wouldn't,' she denied. 'I need to know how I feel, what it is I want.' Halting by her car, she looked up at him, searched his face. 'It was a beautiful night.'

'Yes, it was. Don't make it sound like the end.'

'No.' Unlocking the car door, she added quietly, 'I'll see you in a couple of hours.'

He nodded. 'Drive safely,' he ordered.

Tossing the package containing yesterday's underwear into the back of the car, everything else having been left at the hotel, he closed the car door on her. Watching her reverse out, he gave a last wave, and turned to find Dave waiting for him.

'Food must have been good,' he murmured slyly.

'Mmm,' Nash agreed blandly.

'Must be the longest meal on record.'

'You should try it,' he recommended dismissively as he began strolling round the side of the house.

'Maybe I will.' Absently plucking a budding twig from a bush, he added softly, 'If I can find one like her.'

He didn't answer.

'Who recruited her?'

Nash gave an odd smile. 'I did. I knew her before,' he said casually, and quickly explained why he had contacted her.

'Did she know you'd inherited the Manor? Before you got in touch, I mean?'

About to deny it, he paused. 'It's possible,' he conceded, 'but I don't think so.' Her reaction when she'd climbed from her car and seen him certainly hadn't given the impression of fore-knowledge.

'Any reason for her to bear a grudge?'

'Possibly,' he agreed softly.

'You said you left her at the back of the house whilst you walked out with your architect...'

'Yes.'

'So she *could* have slashed your tyres...'

'Not then,' Nash denied. 'All four tyres were intact when I checked the barn after the window was broken.' But had she been alone after that? He couldn't remember. 'And unless she has an accomplice she couldn't have been responsible for the window.'

'No.' But a seed had been planted.

'Anything happen overnight?'

Dave shook his head. 'No saboteurs creeping around.'

'Perhaps they no longer work nights.' Or perhaps he'd been with the saboteur. 'What did you make of the builder?'

'Marson? Seems honest—but then nearly everyone always does,' he added cynically. 'But I don't think whoever's doing this is intending to hurt anyone, just encourage the building to fall down. And if there hadn't been a sudden property boom, with building land at a premium...'

'Perhaps nothing would have happened.'

'No. And everyone checks out. Everyone here is who they say they are.'

'Matt and Ernie?' he asked. Dave laughed.

'I have someone working on it, to see if they're taking back-handers, and they'll be watched.'

'The developer?'

'Edward Kemp. Clean as a whistle. White as the driven snow.'

'Mmm,' Nash agreed with a smile as disbelieving as Dave's as they continued walking towards the rear perimeter of the property.

'Want me to keep digging?'

'Please.'

'It's going to cost you a fortune.'

'I have a fortune.'

'That's all right, then.' They smiled at each other.

'What are we looking for?' he asked in amusement as Nash continued to scuff the ground with the toe of his shoe as they walked.

'Evidence of this being the front.'

'Sorry?'

Nash smiled. 'One of Miss Langrish's theories. The front of the house was originally at the back. I was looking to see if there was any evidence of a carriage drive or something. It's not important. Have you had any sleep?'

'Don't need much. Like you. I've taken over one of the upper rooms in the east wing. One that actually has a lock and key. There aren't any architectural gems in there,' he grinned, 'so no reason for anyone wanting to poke around. I'll grab sleep as and when I can.'

'Thanks. How's the agency doing?'

'Great. Mostly divorce cases—this makes a nice change. If this was once the front, I imagine there would have been gates onto the main road.'

'Mmm.'

'And if you see a dark-haired chap with a beard he's one of mine.'

Reaching the brick wall at the end, with no sign of any gates having ever been there, they turned and began to walk back. 'Anything else?'

'The surveyor left an envelope for you.' Taking it out of his pocket, he handed it over.

'Thanks.'

Returning to the house, leaving Dave to do whatever it was Dave was doing, Nash went to his room. Settling himself on the bed, he began to read the surveyor's report. It was better than he'd either hoped or expected. Tossing it aside, he lay back and thought about Phoenix. He didn't want her to be sensible, allow her head to rule her heart, but if he were honest with her, told her why he had really left all those years ago, it would probably drive a deeper wedge between them. If it had happened now, he would have handled things very differently, but at twenty-five... Part of the trouble then had been that he *hadn't* wanted his life disrupted. He wanted it disrupted now, and couldn't remember the last time he had viewed life with such anticipation. Just the thought of her made him ache. She couldn't possibly be the saboteur.

In an effort to distract his mind, and his body, he retrieved the surveyor's report and attempted to read it more thoroughly, but he couldn't concentrate.

Feeling restless, he got up and walked into the kitchen complex. After lighting the camping stove, so that he could make a cup of coffee, he turned on the tap to fill the kettle, and the tap fell off. A new tap, which had been fitted only yesterday. There was no sink.

Leaping hastily backwards to avoid the rush of water, he knocked over the stove. An expression on his face seen by few, he righted the stove and turned it out. He had absolutely no idea where the stopcock was.

He rang the plumber, who seemed suitably horrified. Certainly he protested his innocence of shoddy workmanship often enough. Nash neither accused nor reproved, just asked him to mend it. And get rid of all the water.

His mood was no longer benevolent.

CHAPTER FIVE

'SOMEONE'S half sawed through the pipe,' the plumber informed him in apparent bewilderment. 'So that when it was touched...'

'Yes,' agreed Nash, who had also seen the saw marks.

'Why would someone do that?'

'Because someone doesn't want me to restore the Manor. I'll leave you to it.'

Walking out into the sunshine, he stared round him for a moment. *When* had someone sawed through the pipe? The workmen had left at four yesterday, and he'd walked down to the pub with Phoenix. Dave had presumably not needed water after he'd left, otherwise the pipe would have snapped earlier. So it had to be one of the workmen. No one else had been on the property except Dave and his assistant. And Phoenix.

Wandering round the house, unable to find Dave, or his bearded friend, and needing *some* release from his frustration, he began making a systematic search to see if anything else had been tampered with. All he found were Phoenix's glasses, lying on a windowsill. Holding them up to his eyes, he saw that they had slight magnification. He'd been trying so hard *not* to think of Phoenix. It was barely an hour since he'd last seen her, and he missed her.

Deciding he needed some physical activity, he put her glasses in his room and then walked across to the barn to collect the fork he'd seen earlier. He'd decided to look for the courtyard that might or might not have been there.

Completely engrossed with what he was doing, unaware of the passage of time, he was surprised when he saw Phoenix slowly walking round the side of the Manor. She'd changed into a pair of dog-tooth-check trousers and a pink shirt, the sleeves rolled up to her elbows. Her hair was tied back at the nape of her neck.

Catching sight of him, she smiled—and then an expression of alarm crossed her face as she broke into a run.

'What are you *doing*?' she demanded in horror as she stared at the long, deep trench he'd dug.

'Looking for the courtyard.'

'Not like *that*! It has to be done gently! The earth sifted a handful at a time!' Tossing aside the brown envelope she was carrying, she dropped to her knees and began frantically hunting through the mound of soil. 'I can't *believe* you did this! Look at this! *Look!*'

'What?'

Holding up a tiny shard, she exclaimed in anguish, 'It could be an original mosaic!'

'I thought only the Romans laid mosai—'

'Don't argue with me, Nash! Just don't argue with me.' She was frantically brushing the earth off what looked to him like a piece of broken jam jar. He moved his eyes to her face. She looked like a very cross hen.

Wanting very much to laugh, he forced his face into what he hoped was a mask of contrition, although there was nothing contrite about the expression in his eyes. 'I was trying to be helpful,' he murmured.

'Yes! And how many times have I heard *that* before?'

'Is it medieval?' he asked softly, just the merest twitch to his lips.

She obviously yearned to say yes, but, being a truthful girl—or at least he hoped she was truthful—she muttered, 'No.'

'Jam jar?' he asked helpfully.

Expression mutinous, she looked up—and gave a sheepish grin. Tossing away the shard, she admitted, 'Probably, but you still shouldn't be doing it.' Climbing into the trench, she began sliding her hand over the earth wall.

Leaning on the fork, he watched her. 'What are you doing?'

'Looking at soil levels. If there was a court-yard, and if any of it remains, it should show up in a darker line. I can't see anything *obvious*,' she muttered as she continued along the trench, 'but when I've got time I'll mark out the land, try to identify where other buildings might have stood.' Reaching the end, she looked up, and sighed.

'Been thinking again?' he asked sympathetically.

'I wish I could really hate you.'

'I don't.' He held out his hand to help her up. She finally put her own into it, came up quicker than he expected, and he caught her as she tripped on the pile of earth. 'I want to make love to you,' he told her gently. 'It's all I've been able to think about. The way your mouth felt on mine, the way your hands touched me. And the wine,' he whispered. 'Just thinking about it arouses me.'

She shivered. 'I don't want this.'

'You do.' His eyes strayed to her mouth, his hands to her back, and then he kissed her. Thoroughly.

'How charmingly rural,' a low voice drawled mockingly, and he slowly lifted his head to find Chrissie standing not ten feet away. She was nearly as tall as he when wearing high heels. Her long, straight blonde hair was stirring slightly in the breeze. Blue eyes held the same mockery as her voice. And he felt absolutely nothing. His face showed absolutely nothing. Neither did he say anything.

Phoenix stirred in his arms and turned her head.

Still he said nothing.

'A little light comfort?' she asked nastily as she glanced at Phoenix. 'Leave us,' she ordered peremptorily.

Phoenix just looked at her, but she was very still in his arms.

'Very well,' Chrissie finally conceded. Looking back at Nash, she informed him coldly, 'There's a pub just down the road. You can meet me there in five minutes. I won't wait longer.'

Turning on her elegant and probably expensive shoes, she walked away.

'Ex-girlfriend,' he drawled.

Phoenix nodded. 'Model?'

'Yes.'

'Bossy?'

'Yes,' he repeated. 'Interested?'

'It's none of my business.'

'No, nor mine any longer.' But he could see that it was troubling her.

'You aren't going to...?'

'Meet her?' he queried. 'No. What did the archivist have to say?'

Staring at him, she asked, 'And that's it?'

'That's it,' he agreed.

'Ruthless.'

'Sensible. Is that the report?' Indicating the envelope she had dropped earlier, he waited.

Still staring at him, she eventually released herself and went to pick it up. Her back to him, she said, 'My editor friend in London said some thugs tried to rob you not long ago.'

If he was surprised by the change of subject, he didn't show it. 'Yes,' he said noncommittally.

'And that you refused to be robbed.'

Face expressionless, he agreed, 'Yes.'

'There were four of them. With knives.'

'I don't like intimidation.'

'You could have been killed.'

Envelope hugged to her breast, she turned to face him.

'He said you broke the arm of one, the leg of another. The other two ran off, but your hand was badly gashed. A bystander called the police.'

'Yes. Is there a point to all this?'

'Only that one of your attackers said that you didn't say a word when they threatened you, just stared at them. He said he didn't know how anyone could do that. How would I ever get to know you, Nash? If being threatened by a knife doesn't make you talk…'

'Saying please might make me. What does the report say?'

Searching his face again, she said despairingly, 'You don't *want* me to know you, do you?'

'Yes, I do, but telling you about being threatened won't enlighten you. I don't *know* why I'm like I am.'

'And you don't like being questioned.'

He gave a crooked smile. 'No. But then, neither do you.'

She turned away without answering. 'The archivist thinks the house was probably built on the site of a Saxon fort.'

'Does he?' Catching her up, he took her arm. 'Come on, let's go inside and you can tell me all you've found out.'

Leading her into the house, he was astonished to find the plumber still there.

'I'm checking *all* the pipes,' he said grimly.

Nash nodded. 'Did you have time to find out about showers?'

'Yes, and your best bet, if you need one urgently—'

'I do,' Nash put in.

'—is an electric one.'

'Then get me one. As soon as possible?' he asked with a pleasant smile. 'And don't do it on the cheap. If you need money up front, let me know. Don't leave yourself short of funds. I could use a cup of coffee. Do I have water?'

'Yes, sir.'

'Thanks. Sorry to call you out on a Saturday morning.'

The plumber smiled, looked more cheerful. 'I can probably fix you up a shower today,' he began helpfully—or was it hopefully?

'Double time?' Nash asked with a gleam of amusement in his eyes.

'Yes,' he grinned. 'If I take out the old bath...'

'Then do it. When you've made the coffee,' he added with even more amusement. 'I imagine you could do with a cup?'

'Yes.'

'Good. No sugar in mine.' Glancing at Phoenix, he waited, and she said with a rather helpless air, 'Two. Lots of milk.'

Taking her arm, he led her into his room and closed the door. And then he smiled. 'Why are you looking at me like that?'

'Because I've never seen you deal with people before, I suppose. You expect things, and it doesn't seem to occur to you that anyone might refuse.'

'People often refuse,' he argued softly. 'But the plumber needs the work. He has a wife and two small children and very little money. I pay well, Phoenix, but I expect results.'

'Yes,' she agreed quietly. 'Why was he checking all the pipes? I thought he did that yesterday.'

'He did, but someone sawed through one of them.'

'*Sawed* through one of them?' she asked in astonishment. 'When?'

'I don't know. That's why I'm staying here—to find out.' Settling himself more comfortably against the door, he asked quietly, 'Did you know I would be here?'

She didn't *quite* look at him. Neither did she pretend to misunderstand him. 'No,' she denied quietly. 'Neither did I saw through your pipe.' Walking across to the far side of the room, she stared from the narrow window that looked out over the side garden. 'But of all the people here,' she continued softly, 'I am the one who has the best opportunity to sabotage, aren't I? I have a free run of the house, and no one would think anything of me poking and prying, either inside or outside. I obviously didn't break the upstairs window, but I could have an accomplice, couldn't I?'

'Yes. Do you?'

'No.'

'But you live in Oxfordshire…'

'I live in Wiltshire. I'm staying with an old friend from university.'

'But you do know quite a bit about me, don't you?'

'Some. A natural enough curiosity over the years, to see how you were doing. Your name crops up quite often in the papers.'

'Yes.'

There was a soft tap on the door behind him, and he turned to open it. Taking the two mugs of coffee from the plumber, he smiled again. 'Thanks.'

The plumber nodded and walked off.

Pushing the door shut with his foot, he turned to find Phoenix perched on the edge of the bed, her papers spread out in a very businesslike fashion. Carrying the coffees over, he put them on the floor and stood behind her.

'Don't you need your glasses?'

'Yes, but I…'

Walking across to the armchair, he picked them up and handed them to her. 'You left them upstairs yesterday. Other things on your mind, I expect.'

'Yes,' she agreed, without looking at him.

'Don't lie to me, Phoenix, will you?'

She glanced up, mutely shook her head. 'And you won't lie to me, will you? Because you never do.'

'No.'

'Just avoid subjects that might prove thorny.'

Indicating the papers, he ordered quietly, 'Tell me what they say.'

Putting on her glasses, she began to read. 'When William the Conqueror made his great survey of 1066, he noted that Peter de Teyne was the chief landowner at Mincotte—note the different spelling...'

'Yes.'

Her voice constrained, she continued, 'And then a charter of 1216 mentions a Henry Oddly as landowner.'

When he didn't answer, she put down her papers with a gentle sigh.

'Mistrust and jealousy play havoc with the emotions, don't they?'

'Yes, but *you* have nothing to be jealous of.'

'Neither do you, but I meant *your* mistrust. Because you do mistrust me, don't you? You aren't entirely sure of my motives.'

'Not entirely,' she agreed. 'Aren't you interested in how the Manor got its name?'

'I'm more interested in why you're avoiding the issue of Chrissie.'

'I'm not. She looks like a first-class bitch.' Turning over the papers, she continued flatly, 'It seems likely that the settlement was chosen for its proximity to a nearby ford.'

'What ford?' he asked softly, his eyes on her profile.

She shrugged. 'There must have been one across the river.'

'The Cherwell?'

'I suppose. And here...' Dragging another piece of paper towards her, she continued, 'It says that Mincott Oddly was included in the parish until 1840, when the church was built. I also discovered that someone called Damis sold it for £1,200 in 1842 to a family named Bessiton. So, we're making progress.'

'Are we?'

'Yes.'

'But intimacy isn't to be thought of at the moment, is it?' he murmured softly. 'Because an ex-girlfriend showed up.'

'And you seem to think I'm a saboteur,' she countered.

'A passing thought that you *could* be one. My body says no, but my mind doesn't *quite* dismiss the possibility. Do you know an Edward Kemp?'

She gave an odd smile. 'No, Nash, I don't know anyone named Edward Kemp.' Slowly tidying her papers together, she added thoughtfully, 'It's odd, isn't it? Our bodies know each other, but our minds are poles apart. A strange feeling to be intimate with someone you don't know.'

'Yes.'

'And I think,' she began firmly, 'that until we know each other we shouldn't...'

'Make love?'

'Yes. Who finished with who?'

'Chrissie finished with me. She walked out to teach me a lesson.'

'Did you learn it?'

'Not the lesson she wanted me to.' Sitting beside her, he took the papers out of her hand and tossed them towards the armchair. Removing her glasses, he tossed them in the same direction. Holding her eyes, he asked gently, 'What is it *you* want me to learn?'

'Who I am. *What* I am. Chrissie really is history?'

'Yes.'

'I wanted to scratch her eyes out.'

'She has that effect on a lot of people,' he said drily. 'And I wish, more than anything, that I had been your first lover.'

Startled, she looked down. 'So do I,' she whispered softly.

'Do you?' he asked gently.

'Yes.'

He found himself wanting to say that he would be her last, but he didn't, because he didn't know her. Touching his fingers to her exquisite face, he gently kissed her. 'I need a shower.'

'Nash…' she protested.

'Shh. There's an inevitability about it, Phoenix. Last night we both wanted what we missed out on ten years ago. And now I want you again. Perhaps I will always want you.' Gently laying her back on the bed, he touched his mouth to hers, felt the kick his body gave, the arousal that was never far away. 'Not the most ideal surroundings to make love to you,' he murmured. 'Dave is somewhere around, and the plumber…'

She didn't answer, just stared at him, her wide, dark eyes filled with helpless desire. 'I could tack a blanket up at the window—except I don't have any blankets.' He smiled as he began to kiss her.

'Lock the door,' she murmured huskily.

'No lock.' Her breathing was accelerating in the most satisfying way. So was his. Moving one hand downwards, he untucked her shirt from her trousers, put his warm palm on her ribcage—and jumped as there was an almighty crash from the front of the house.

They both stiffened. Nash rolled free and was out of the door before Phoenix had even drawn breath.

Shoving open the double doors that led through to the east wing, he saw the shattered window and the rock lying in the middle of the floor, then quickly turned as Dave came thundering down the stairs.

He grasped the shaky banister, lost his balance, and was forced to jump the last three stairs. 'Someone ought to mend that... Know anyone with a red sports car? I just had time to see it accelerating away.'

Staring at Dave, he gave a grim smile. Sharp thinking and Phoenix clearly didn't mix. Striding back to his room, he met Phoenix just coming out. Lifting her to one side, he picked up his mobile from the armchair and quickly punched out his secretary's home number. He hadn't even queried how Chrissie had known where he was.

'Jane? It's Nash. Get on to a locksmith and get him to change the locks on my apartment, will you? Yes, now. And instruct the security guard that he is not to let Miss Lane into my apartment under any circumstances. Keep one set of keys for yourself and give one set to Security. Thanks.' After listening for a moment, he answered, 'I'll come down later and sign them. Leave them in my desk at home.'

Disconnecting, he turned to find both Phoenix and Dave in the doorway watching him.

'You'll need another glazier,' Dave said laconically.

'Yes.'

'Chrissie drives a red sports car?' Phoenix asked quietly.

'Yes.'

'What will you do?'

'Don't ask,' Dave laughed. 'It's sometimes best not to know what Nash is intending to do. Anyone want a coffee?'

As Dave turned away to walk to the kitchen Nash looked at Phoenix, and he could see very clearly that she *did* want to know what he was intending to do.

'Let her know she was seen,' he said quietly. 'She isn't very bright sometimes. She's angry because I won't play her games,' he explained at her puzzled look. 'I'm surprised she's waited this long to gain some revenge.' And this had to be the first time he'd ever explained himself to anyone.

'Will she stop at smashing windows?'

'I doubt it. The newspapers will probably be her next stop.'

'But if you let her know she was seen you can discredit her in turn?'

'She'll think I will, because that's the way her mind works. And top models can't afford adverse publicity. I'd better ring the glazier.'

When he'd done that, he rang Jane back and asked her to inform Chrissie's agency of what she had done. And to tell them to warn her off.

'Because you'll play dirtier than she will?' Phoenix asked quietly when he'd disconnected.

He didn't answer. He probably didn't need to.

Dave came back just then and asked, 'Why are the plumber's tools in the kitchen and the floor wet?'

After explaining, Nash asked, 'Were you here all the time I was out yesterday and last night?'

'Apart from about an hour when I went out to get something to eat. My colleague was covering.'

Nash merely nodded.

'No one could have got in last night,' he insisted.

'So it had to have been done whilst the workmen were here.'

'Yes. I'll do some more checking.'

When he'd returned to the kitchen, Phoenix said quietly, 'I'm a distraction you don't need, aren't I?'

He gave a wry smile. 'Mmm.'

'Want me to leave?'

'No, but maybe you should, for your own safety.'

'I have insurance.'

'Who's the beneficiary?' he quipped.

She smiled. 'My mum.'

'How is she?' He'd liked her mother. It had been her father he couldn't stand.

Her smile widened. 'After Dad died...'

'When?'

'Five years ago. Mum sold the house and bought a cottage. She paints dreadful pictures,' she said fondly, 'wears a battered old fishing hat she found in a jumble sale, and has a dog called Rover.'

'Original,' he smiled.

'And I've never seen her so happy.'

He wasn't surprised. He didn't imagine her life had been very fulfilling married to Phoenix's father. But he wished he'd known, maybe then he would have contacted her five years earlier.

A tapping on the window made them both jump. Turning, they saw Mike, hands at either side of his face, peering in at them.

'Well, there goes my big seduction scene,' Nash said wryly, 'and, judging by your face, perhaps it's just as well?'

'Yes.'

'And the surroundings aren't exactly salubrious, are they?' he murmured as he glanced sadly round. 'Pity it was empty for so long.'

'How long?'

'Fifteen years, and although the villagers have been keeping an eye on the place since the old boy who rented the Manor from my aunt died a great deal of damage has been done. There was, apparently, a beautiful carpet in the front room, but the front window was blown in during a storm and it got soaked. Possibly it could have been restored, but the villagers flung it out. Along with the one on the landing. Same thing, same storm—and here comes Mike,' he added all in the same breath as his friend shoved open the door.

'Front window's broken,' he began, and both Nash and Phoenix smiled at him.

He gave an embarrassed grin. 'More sabotage?'

'Chrissie,' Nash said drily.

'*Chrissie?* You haven't had *another* row, have you?' he demanded in exasperation. 'She sounded perfectly friendly when I spoke to her this morn... What?' he demanded comically.

Nash leaned against the wall and folded his

arms. 'When I want someone to know where I am,' he drawled, 'I will tell them.'

'But I didn't!'

'Sorry?'

'I didn't tell her,' he insisted. 'I mean, what with...' Glancing meaningfully at Phoenix and back to his friend, he continued, 'She *asked* me where you were, and I said I didn't know.'

'Then who did tell her?' asked Nash softly, almost to himself.

'I don't know.'

'No,' Nash agreed with a small smile. 'And I don't have rows,' he tacked on softly. 'Are those my plans?'

'What? Oh, yes.' Brandishing the roll of paper he was carrying, he looked round for somewhere to put them.

'Use the bed—it isn't likely to be used for anything else at the moment,' he added, too softly for Mike to hear. But Phoenix heard, and she gave an enchanting blush.

'Can I see?' she asked as Mike unrolled his plans on the bed.

'Only if you don't interfere,' Nash told her.

Two hours later—hours of arguing, discussing, altering—they finally had a workable plan.

'Right,' said Mike. 'I'll need to check measurements before I finalise them...'

'And I need something to eat,' Nash murmured. 'Lend me your car keys; I'll go and get a take-away.'

'And I'll go back to hacking off plaster,' Phoenix added.

'Chipping,' Nash corrected her. 'Hack and you're dead.'

She laughed and went out.

As soon as she was out of earshot, Mike murmured, 'Are you and Phoenix…er…you know?'

Nash merely smiled, appropriated Mike's car keys and walked out.

When he returned, carrying hamburgers and chips for all of them, because it was the only place he could find open, it was to see Phoenix entering the front door carrying a black bin liner.

'You've found a body?' he asked in amusement.

'No,' she laughed. 'It's to carry out the plaster I've been ha…chipping off.'

'Leave it for the builders. And what on earth is Mike doi——? Mind!' he yelled as the head of the hammer Mike was wielding suddenly flew off towards Phoenix.

CHAPTER SIX

SHOVING Phoenix out of the way with his shoulder, he watched the hammer head strike the wall beside the front door and the plaster spider web into a thousand cracks.

Mike looked frozen halfway up the stairs, the shaft of the hammer still in his hand like a baton. Phoenix was crouched over, a hand to her face.

Dumping the food on the bottom stair, Nash went to her. 'Show me. Are you hurt?'

'No,' she denied shakily as she straightened. 'Do you think someone's trying to kill me?' Staring at him, she whispered, 'The window upstairs, the stone outside the back door, and now this.'

'Yes,' he agreed grimly. 'I want you out of here.'

'No.'

'Is she all right? Are you all right?' Mike asked worriedly. 'Dear God, Phoenix, I could have killed you.'

'Not your fault,' she reassured him. 'I thought carpenters were supposed to look after their tools.'

'What were you doing?' Nash asked him.

'Mending the banister. Dave said he'd nearly broken his neck earlier, and when I grasped it just now... The carpenter had left his tool bag and so I borrowed his hammer.'

Nash bent to pick up the head, and, as though it were just the prompt it had been waiting for, there was a slithering sound, followed by a thump, and a cloud of dust rose to surround them.

Turning, all three stared at the wall. Now minus most of the plaster.

'I should have sold to the developers,' Nash murmured sadly.

'Don't be silly,' Phoenix derided. 'They would have pulled the house down...'

'Yes,' he agreed wistfully.

'And there might even be panelling under there,' she began eagerly as she took a step towards the walls.

Grasping her arm, he said decisively, 'There is *not* any panelling under there.'

'But...'

'No.' Firmly turning her in the direction of the staircase, he pointed at the take-away. 'Eat.' Catching a movement from the corner of his eye, he lifted his head and saw Dave hovering on the half-landing.

'What happened?' he asked quietly as he descended.

'The head flew off the hammer and cracked the plaster. I got you burger and chips.'

'Thanks.'

'Know any good plasterers?'

He smiled. It looked rather strained, Nash noticed. Understandable, he supposed. He probably felt responsible because he hadn't yet found out who was sabotaging the place.

They all sat on the staircase to eat, all looking at the wall. No one said anything about an accident. And why had the carpenter left his tools? Nash wondered. Didn't craftsmen guard them with their lives? Didn't they check their hammers before they used them? Mike wouldn't, of course; he would have had no reason to. He thought it was time to pay a visit to the developers. Personally.

'When's your expert coming to drill out the infills from the bar tracery?' he asked Phoenix.

'Monday.'

He nodded. 'Then I think I'll drive down to London this afternoon. I have some business to take care of. You go and do some more research.'

'But I want to...'

'No,' he denied gently. 'I don't want you here in the house on your own.'

'But I won't be on my own. Dave will be here…'

'Don't argue,' he said dismissively. 'Mike, can you be ready to apply for planning permission for the kitchen area and the landing by Monday?'

'Yes,' he agreed.

'OK. I'll instruct Marson to get on with the roof.'

Phoenix gave an ironic little clap. 'Thank you, everyone, for your attention. Dismissed.'

Nash merely looked at her.

'Pay for that, will I?' she asked softly, with a little gleam of laughter in her eyes.

'Mmm.' And he wanted to kiss her. Make love to her here on the stairs. And he didn't think he cared *who* was watching. Something of his thoughts must have shown in his face, because she went pink and looked hastily away. Must be slipping, he thought wryly; no one could usually see *anything* from his face. Or so he'd been told.

Popping the last chip into his mouth—and he truly didn't think he had ever eaten a meal quite so tasteless—he screwed up the paper bag and got to his feet. Waited for everyone else to do the same with a small smile on his mouth.

He saw Phoenix and Mike out to their cars,

waited until they were out of sight before returning to have a word with Dave, and then walked down to the village to collect his own car.

He used the time driving down to Kensington to think long and hard about every aspect of the sabotage. Every person who could possibly be involved. He had a great many suspicions, but no proof. And all these little accidents were beginning to annoy him.

Collecting the new set of keys from the security guard, he let himself into his apartment. After opening windows to let in some fresh air, he showered and shaved, changed into clean clothes, and then settled himself at his desk in his study. He signed the papers Jane had left for him, then leaned back and put his feet up on the desk, his expression thoughtful. Finally pulling a pad towards him, he began to make notes—and then he made some phone calls. One of them to his wine supplier, asking them to deliver a dozen bottles of malt whisky to Don.

Early on Monday morning he rang Edward Kemp and asked to see him. Kemp didn't refuse. He hadn't expected that he would. The meeting went more or less as he'd expected. Not as Edward Kemp had expected, but then, that hadn't been his intention.

He drove back to Mincott Oddly, parked his

car in Don's drive, and saw Phoenix over on the green playing rounders, or baseball, with some of the boys from the village. And *this* was the real Phoenix, he thought as he continued to watch her—all long legs and enthusiasm. The Phoenix he remembered from ten years ago. She gave the ball an almighty whack, dropped the bat, and ran, long legs flying. Her laughter carried clearly on the still air as she made it to the last base and threw herself down. Rolling onto her back, she stared up at the blue sky. And that was the Phoenix he wanted back. The one his heart ached for. But he didn't know if she was saint or saboteur. Occasionally, far *too* occasionally, she forgot to be wary with him, but then she would presumably remember that he had walked out on her ten years before, and she'd try to make her head rule her heart. But did her head rule her enough to make her a saboteur? He didn't know.

Turning away, face sombre, he was about to post his keys through Don's letter-box when he opened the door.

'Lovely girl,' Don commented, which only went to prove that he had been watching Nash whilst Nash watched Phoenix.

'Yes,' he agreed.

'Always got a word and a smile for everyone when she comes down to the village. Thought you might like to bring her to the village fête on Saturday.'

'Did you?' Nash asked drily.

'Yes. Starts at ten.'

'Don't be late?'

'Something like that. Found your saboteur yet?'

Nash shook his head.

'Won't be anyone from the village.'

'No,' Nash agreed. 'I didn't think it was.'

'Ed—the plumber...'

'I know who Ed is.'

'He was worried you might think it was him.'

'I didn't.' Handing over his keys, he turned away.

'See you Saturday,' Don called after him. It wasn't a question.

A faint smile on his face, Nash walked to the Manor.

The tarpaulin was off the roof of the east wing, he saw, and he could see several figures up there working. A long chute ran down the side of the house to take the rubble, and a skip sat proudly on his lawn. Grass, he mentally substituted. Phoenix's car was parked up near the barn, and he sighed. He wanted her. Despite what she might have done, despite what she might be, he wanted her. His heart quickened when he thought of her, and the memory of the feel of her was driving him insane. But he didn't know if he could trust her, and that bothered him a great deal. But as far as he could see there were only two candidates for saboteur, and she was one of them.

Walking through the open front door, he climbed up to the half-landing, idly traced the ancient window that she had exposed. He didn't know how long he stood there—not long he thought—before he heard her soft footsteps in the hall below.

Turning, he stared down at her, watched her climb towards him. She looked extraordinarily troubled, a vast contrast to how she'd been a few minutes before. Please don't let it be her, he prayed. But he had an awful sinking feeling that it was.

'Hello,' she said quietly.

'Hello. You're looking very thoughtful,' he murmured as he bent to kiss her. 'Expert not turned up yet?'

She shook her head. 'Nash?'

'Mmm?' he answered idly as he rubbed a nubble of plaster off with his thumb.

'Nothing,' she denied quickly. 'It isn't important.'

'It might be,' he argued softly. 'Tell me any way.'

'No, I...' She was silent for a few minutes, then finally continued, somewhat evasively, he thought, 'I had a look at the surveyor's report you left in your room.'

Disappointed, because he didn't think that was what she had originally intended to say, he murmured, 'And?'

'And so, just out of curiosity, and because of the things that have been happening, I went to check on all the things he'd listed as broken or needing attention.'

'And?' he repeated as he found another nubble to remove.

'And now they're broken even more.'

'Ah. Do I have a shower?'

'Yes,' she agreed, her face puzzled. 'Don't you care?'

He looked down at her, smiled. 'Yes, Phoenix, I care. Come and show me the shower.'

She hesitated a moment, still staring at him, and then a look of almost defiance crossed her face. Turning abruptly, she led the way up the remaining stairs and along the landing to the bathroom. Pushing open the door, she stood back to allow him to look inside.

He did so, then laughed. 'There would be more

room in a telephone box—and decent paving round it.' Staring at the cracked and torn lino that, presumably, the plumber had made some attempt to clean, he shook his head. 'How the mighty are fallen—and stop looking at me like that.'

'You aren't looking at me to know I'm looking at you like anything,' she protested.

'I can feel you.' Turning his head, he smiled with his eyes. 'Does it work?'

'I imagine so. Nash…?'

He kissed her into silence and urged her inside. Shutting the door with his elbow, he pulled her close. 'Kiss me?'

She didn't answer.

'I'll take that as an affirmative. Kiss me hello.' His voice thicker, even against his will, he felt his body change, his eyes darken. Such a beautiful face, he thought.

'You're different,' she said quietly.

'I'm deprived.' Bending his head, he closed his eyes and kissed her, hard and long, felt the quiver she gave, the melting of her body against his. A reluctant melting? he wondered. A reaction she could no more help than he could? Thoughts momentarily suspended, he gave in to bliss.

Sliding his hands beneath the short-sleeved

sweater she wore, he touched the warmth of her back and gave a small shiver as her hands found the warm flesh of his own back.

Gently resting her against the wall, he leaned into her, and breathing became difficult. Grazing his mouth across her scented skin, he rested a moment at her neck, touched his tongue to the throbbing cord there. Her hands were clenched against his spine, her legs slightly splayed as she accepted the warmth of him against her.

Moving his hands to her ribs, he rested his thumbs beneath the underside of her full breasts, felt them swell. With a groan he couldn't suppress, he leaned slightly away and tugged her top up and over her head. She gasped, then rested her hands on his chest, her breathing erratic.

As she stared up at him, her eyes deep and dark, almost black in the dim room, mouth slightly parted, something changed in her expression. Not hardness exactly, but deliberation, almost as though she would use him for her own ends. And then she began to undo the buttons on his shirt.

He unhooked her bra and she obediently removed one arm and then the other.

Eyes holding eyes, she leaned slightly forward until her breasts brushed his naked chest—and even through the blurring of desire, of knowing something was different, he didn't stop.

Experienced and capable, he nevertheless fumbled slightly as he undid her jeans and then his own, and the deliberation of both actions somehow heightened senses already heightened, aroused desire that was already nearly out of control as they brought each other to a gasping climax.

Breathing laboured, they leant against each other in shock.

Her skin felt clammy and shivery. But then, so did his. And he couldn't quite believe that his self-control had slipped so badly.

Smoothing his palms up and down her arms, he finally allowed them to rest at her neck and tilted her face up to his.

She stared at him as though numb, and then she slowly touched her fingers to his mouth. Her lips looked swollen from his kisses. His own felt the same. And that in itself was arousing.

Touching his tongue to her lower lip, he felt her shiver. Moved it to her teeth, her tongue, and the desire began all over again.

He didn't remember ever kissing someone with such monumental passion, such a blurring, mindless desire as he kissed Phoenix. Had never known a female body to fit quite so exquisitely to his own, or ever felt the warmth she generated, the sheer excitement, and he wanted to bury himself inside her, and only restrained himself with a sheer physical effort that hurt.

Her neck was bent at an impossible angle across his forearm, his fingers tangled in her thick hair. His other hand was free to roam her warm curves, touch where he wanted to touch as she quivered against him, vulnerable and weak. He had total power at that moment, he thought, and it frightened him to death.

'You could destroy me,' he said thickly against her mouth. 'And I wouldn't even put up a fight.'

She took a deep breath, and opened her eyes. She looked drugged. 'Yes, you would,' she argued huskily. 'If you really thought I was destroying you, you would walk away and not look back. I'm trying for the same courage,' she admitted honestly. 'Trying to use you for my own ends, but...'

'But it doesn't work, does it?'

'No,' she agreed thickly. 'Because my hands remember your flesh, my mind your power. I tell myself over and over that I don't want this. But I do,' she admitted on a trembling sigh. 'The dear God knows I do.' Fingers digging into his shoulders, she added emotionally, 'When you touch me I can't breathe, can't think; all I can do is hold on and hope not to drown. My heart feels bruised.'

'So does mine. And I've forgotten how to laugh.'

To his surprise, her eyes filled with tears that trembled on her lashes and then spilled slowly down her face. And he didn't want to ask what he should ask. For the first time in his life, he didn't want an answer. And so he kissed her again, and then slowly disentangled himself, forced himself to smile. It felt extraordinarily shaky. 'If there's a better time to try out the shower, I can't think of it.'

'No. I wanted to be in control,' she whispered, 'and you've just proved what a mockery that is. Don't hurt me, Nash,' she pleaded. 'Please don't hurt me.'

'Not intentionally. Not ever that.' And if he asked, and if she was honest, told him what he suspected, he didn't think he could live with it. Not now. Not today. And he remembered despising a friend who'd loved a fool.

They took it in turns to shower, and there was only one small hand towel to dry themselves with. They didn't look at each other as they dressed.

When they returned to the landing, it was to

find her expert had arrived and was busily removing infills. Nash left Phoenix with him and went to find Dave, who was in his room.

'Anything been happening?'

'No,' he denied quietly, 'but whoever's doing this I don't think it's the property developer. It's not his style.'

'No,' agreed Nash, who knew very well that it wasn't the property developer.

'The original attempts at demolition haven't been touched again. These are small things, irritating things, but not meant to destroy the house.'

'No.'

'Someone who doesn't like you.'

'Yes.'

'Someone who works here, or someone paying someone who works here.'

'Yes.'

'How many enemies do you have?'

He gave a wry smile. 'Quite a few, I imagine.'

'And whoever it is is making you spend more money than you need. Annoying you, irritating you, getting their own back. Any ideas?'

'One or two. I'll think about it.'

'Then think quickly. I can't do much unless I have a name. Not much point in me staying until...'

'Yes, there is. I need you to watch.'

'Fair enough. Just thought I ought to mention it.'

By the end of the week he had plaster on most walls, some new roof beams on the east wing, leaded glass infills on his bar tracery, a new bathroom suite, tiles on the bathroom floor and a door knocked through into one newly decorated bedroom. A carpet had been chosen and would be fitted the following week. Bed and bedding would be delivered soon after.

He had mounds of earth at the rear of the Manor, where Phoenix was busily looking for traces of old buildings and a courtyard, and a kitchen he could still barely use until planning permission came through, but he could get decorators in to make some of the rooms habitable.

Standing on the landing, with its bizarre patchwork of newly exposed beams, courtesy of Phoenix, he stared from the window and watched her bang in her little pegs to mark out the courtyard. She was wearing shorts, and he wanted her with a dull ache that wouldn't go away. They hadn't made love again since the incident in the bathroom, as though both had silently made a pact to be sensible. He didn't want to be sensible. Neither did he want the workmen staring at her long legs, which they were. Who could help it? They were terrific legs. And a terrific backside, which was shown to advantage when she knelt down, which she did every time she banged in a peg.

Nothing else had happened. No more little acts of sabotage. He didn't know if that was significant or not. Perhaps whoever it was had given up.

Moving slowly down the back staircase, he walked out into the grounds and up behind her.

Aware that he was watched by envious eyes, because he had made it very clear that watching Phoenix was *all* the workmen were allowed to do, he said quietly, 'It's the village fête tomorrow.' And she jumped, turned quickly round. She looked wary. 'We have to be there at ten.'

'We?'

'Yes. I shall need moral support.'

Slowly straightening, the mallet clutched in her hand, she said quietly, 'I don't know if I'm moral.'

'Don't you?'

She shook her head.

'Come anyway.'

'All right.'

'Don't wear shorts. They scramble my brain,'

he explained at her look of query. 'And the brain of every other male in the vicinity.'

Glancing quickly up at the house, and no doubt seeing the workmen watching her, as he had done, she looked as quickly away.

'I want you,' he added softly. And she closed her eyes, almost in defeat, he thought.

'I thought physical activity would...'

'But it doesn't, does it?' he asked gently.

'No,' she agreed huskily.

'And you still don't trust me, do you?'

'Trust you?' she echoed warily.

'Mmm, enough to tell me the truth.'

Looking down, she fiddled with the mallet. 'What truth is that?'

Disappointed, he shook his head. 'It doesn't matter. I'll see you tomorrow.' Turning away, he walked down to the village to collect his car and drive to London. Because he didn't think he could stay.

A village fête, he thought wryly as he stared from his apartment window on Saturday morning, and, this being England, as soon as any kind of sport was scheduled, or a garden party, or a fête, the weather changed. After weeks of blue sky, warm sun, they now had grey clouds, a blustery wind and spots of rain.

He dressed appropriately and drove to Mincott Oddly. With a wry smile for the sight of rain-slick marquees set up on the green, dripping fairground rides for the children, stalls that were being pegged hastily down in the swirling wind, he drove on to the Manor and found Phoenix waiting for him. She was back in her jeans and sturdy shoes, a waxed jacket round her shoulders, and he yearned to see her in a pretty dress. Wanted to take her out, show her off. Climbing from the car, he bent to kiss her. She tasted of raindrops.

He held the car door open for her, then drove into the village and parked, as usual, at Don's. He didn't think he'd ever been to a fête in his life. A new experience for him. Phoenix seemed to know everyone, and waved and chatted as they threaded their way through the sparse crowds, but she wasn't happy, and her voice sounded false and strained.

'You aren't entering into the spirit of the thing,' she reproved quietly as they passed yet another game where he could have tried his skill. 'All proceeds go towards the church roof.'

'I have a roof of my own.'

'Then hold a fête.'

Halting her, he turned her to look at him. Even with wet hair she looked beautiful, but extraordinarily sad. 'What's wrong?'

'Nothing. Let's go and look at the old skills tent. They show you thatching, and, well, other things. How to make a willow fence.'

'Useful.'

'Stop it!' she hissed fiercely. 'They want so *badly* for you to fit in! Don't you *know* that?'

Startled, he watched her stride towards the skills tent. Catching her up, he turned her again, and she wrenched free. 'This won't *work*, Nash!' And she sounded and looked so despairing that his heart ached.

'Why won't it?'

'Because I can't forget! I've tried and tried, but I can't.'

'Forget what? That I walked out on you?'

'No!' she denied in anguish. 'That my father paid you to do so.'

CHAPTER SEVEN

STUNNED, he just stared at her, and then she was gone. Fleet as a deer, she ran between the booths and was gone.

So that was why she hadn't begged or pleaded all those years ago—no, not begged, because that wasn't her style, but he might have expected that she would ask if they would meet again when he got back from the States. She hadn't. Now he knew why. And why heart and head were in such conflict.

'Mr Vallender?'

Expression blank, he turned to stare at Lally Watkins junior.

'The vicar would like to meet you.'

The vicar? he thought hollowly. Urgency driving him, he said quickly, 'I'll be back in a minute.' Without waiting for an answer, he sprinted after Phoenix. He caught her just as she reached the Manor house and her car.

'No,' she begged tearfully.

'Yes.'

'And you aren't even *breathing* hard,' she accused.

'No. Phoenix,' he began gently as he stared down into her tear- and rain-washed face, 'I didn't take money from your father.'

'He said you did.'

'He lied.'

'No,' she denied in despair. 'Let me go, Nash.'

'No. I can't let you go. Not this time.'

She closed her eyes and he wanted to lick those rain-damp lashes, hold her warmly in his arms and never let her go. Without even knowing he was going to say it, he begged so very gently, 'Marry me.'

And she burst into tears.

Gathering her in his arms, he gently rocked her.

When she'd quietened, he gave her his handkerchief and she blew her nose hard, like a little girl. 'I have to go away,' she said on a shuddery breath. 'I have to think. Let me go now.'

'Only if you promise to come back. Give me your word, Phoenix, and I'll let you go.'

'All right,' she whispered, 'I give you my word.'

'And you'll come back in a few days.'

'A week.'

'No, a few days. Look at me.' When she looked up, he added, 'Promise?'

She gave a jerky nod.

'If you don't, I'll find you. I *will* find you.'

'I'll come back,' she agreed. 'And now you have to go back to the fête.'

He shook his head.

'Yes,' she insisted. 'You must. They want you to belong, Nash. Please?'

He gave a crooked smile. 'All right.'

'And be nice to them—patient. Promise?'

'I promise.'

Eyes still tear-washed, she murmured huskily, 'I'm going now.'

'All right.'

Opening the car door for her, he waited for her to climb inside, and then gently closed it. He couldn't make her stay, couldn't force her; he had to give her time. Hard as it was to allow her to leave looking so tragic, he had to give her time.

When she'd gone, he reluctantly returned to the fête. To find his gardener still waiting for him with the elderly vicar.

He forced a smile, apologised for rushing off, and they shook hands. Stifling impatience, he allowed himself to be regaled with a potted history of the village and the state of the church, to be asked whether he was a churchgoer, and could they expect to see him there some time soon, and whether he was going to live permanently in the village.

'I knew your aunt,' the vicar continued, and then he frowned. 'Would you mind if we got out of this wind and rain? My arthritis, you know.'

'No, of course not.' Steering the vicar towards the refreshment tent, Nash bought them both a cup of tea and sat with him at a small rickety table. Only vaguely listening, he thought about Phoenix. He should never have allowed her to drive in that state.

'No need to look so troubled,' the vicar protested, 'and it's not as bad as that, but still...'

'Sorry?'

'But I can see you're a man who thinks as I do—that the Lord's house isn't really the place for groups.'

'Groups?'

'Yes, but if it helps the attendance...'

'Yes.' Dragging his mind back, and without the faintest idea what the vicar was talking about, he sipped his tea and forced himself to concentrate.

'Youngsters want other things now, don't they?' he queried sadly. 'Not like in your aunt's time.'

'No. What was she like?'

'Didn't you know her?' he asked in surprise.

'No, I hadn't met her since I was a child.' And, if truth be told, he had almost forgotten her existence.

The vicar happily launched into reminiscences and Nash was free to let his mind wander again. Where had she gone? Oxford? Or back to Wiltshire? Smiling automatically, and nodding every time the vicar finished another anecdote, he suddenly felt guilty. He *should* be listening, should want to know what his aunt had been like, but at the moment all he could think about was Phoenix.

Cutting into the vicar's monologue, he said gently, 'I don't think you should be sitting here in damp clothes. Why don't I come and see you at the vicarage one evening? Then we can talk in comfort.' The old man's face lit up with such pleasure that he felt even more guilty.

Putting down his unwanted tea, he got to his feet, but before he could help the vicar up Lally Watkins junior rushed up and did it for him. 'I'll take him back to the vicarage, Mr Vallender.'

'Thank you.'

'Come on, sir. Mum'll have the kettle on and something hot to eat.'

He patted the young man's arm, smiled sweetly at Nash, almost pleaded, 'You won't forget?' and, when Nash shook his head, walked away on young Lally's arm.

'Getting frail,' Don said from beside him.

'Yes.'

'Seventy-nine, he is. The village is his life. Tuesday evening is a good time to visit him. Sun's trying to come out.'

Turning to look up at the still leaden sky, and then at Don, he asked drily, 'Is it?'

'Yes. You haven't had a go on anything.'

'Biding my time,' he said, even more drily. 'I don't believe in rushing into anything.' Except intimacy with Phoenix. Had he really asked her to marry him? Yes, because it was what he wanted. He didn't care what she might or might not have done; he only knew that he wanted her with him for the rest of his life. If she would have him.

'Miss Langrish had to leave?'

'Yes,' Nash agreed quietly. 'She had an appointment.'

And no man had greater love, he later thought tiredly, than one who systematically sampled every marquee at the fair, shied every coconut, fished every duck, and all because someone had said he should.

He stayed to the end, until tired, over-excited children had been dragged home by their parents, until the cake stall had run out of cakes, and then he began walking back to the Manor.

'Mr Vallender!'

Reluctantly halting, he turned, saw a red-faced man hurrying towards him dragging a teenage boy. He stared at Nash for a moment, then thrust the boy forward and said angrily, 'Go on, tell him!'

The boy glared, then looked down. 'Sorry,' he muttered.

'What for?' Nash asked mildly.

'Breaking your window.'

'Which window?'

'The bloody window at the back!' Then he staggered as the man grabbed his shoulder and shook him.

'You swear again and I'll take my belt to you.'

'It's not allowed,' he sneered.

'Isn't it?' he demanded grimly. 'You carry on like this and you'll find out *just* what's allowed.' Turning back to Nash, he explained, 'Took my shotgun, didn't they? Him and that tearaway Jason took the key to the gun cabinet. But I didn't know they'd broken your window. Didn't find *that* out until just now. Overheard him telling Jason you were the one who came out to look.'

'Well, I didn't do it on purpose!' the boy insisted. 'It was an accident. We were shooting at a bird on the roof.'

'That still doesn't excuse the fact that you took the gun without permission! I trusted you!'

Weary of the argument, Nash stared at the lad until he was forced to look away. 'There was a young woman on the landing,' he said quietly, 'standing right in front of that window. If either pellets or glass had hit her, she could have been disfigured for life. I shall expect you to pay for the window. Yourself. If you don't have any money you can work off the debt at the Manor. The glazier's name is Dodson. He's in the book. He'll tell you how much you owe. And you can apologise to Miss Langrish when you see her.' *If* you see her, he mentally added.

'Phoenix? Bloody hell, I like her!'

'I'm very glad to hear it.' Turning to the boy's father—at least, he assumed it was his father—he added, 'Thank you for telling me.'

With an abrupt nod, he continued on his way to the Manor. And *that* was what had been puzzling him. No one had been at the Manor when the window had been broken except himself and Phoenix. And unless she'd had an accomplice she could not have been responsible. But she could have been responsible for everything else. *Could* have, but he no longer thought so.

Hair soaked, trousers soaked, shoes caked in mud, he reached the Manor just as the sun *did* come out. And he discovered why someone had originally covered up his bar tracery. The dying sun shone straight through it, blinding anyone who walked in the front door.

Squinting, turning his head to one side, he went to look for Dave.

He found him in his room, and as Nash walked in with only a peremptory knock Dave looked up, startled, and hastily scored through the paper he was holding.

Recovering quickly, he said, 'You don't look entirely fulfilled by your day at the fair.'

'No,' Nash replied. Walking across the dusty room, he tweaked the paper out of Dave's hand. 'What's this? A progress report?'

Hastily trying to grab it back, and failing, he said irritably, 'No. I have a page on everyone who's been here...'

'And this is Miss Langrish's.' Taking it across to the window, he began to read.

'It's only a list of her movements,' Dave insisted hastily, 'nothing incriminating...'

'And methinks the man protests too much,' Nash said softly, but with such steel in his voice that Dave was momentarily silenced.

'It isn't her,' he finally insisted.

Glancing up, Nash asked quietly, 'Because you don't want it to be?'

'Nothing's happened this last week.'

'No. But of everyone working here she's had the best opportunity for sabotage, hasn't she? The fact that no one wants it to be her doesn't alter the facts.'

'They aren't facts,' Dave insisted. 'And there's no proof. Nothing major was done, nothing life-threatening.'

'Just expensive,' Nash said softly. 'And time-consuming.'

'But why would Phoenix do *anything*? She loves this house. Wants it restored. And she couldn't have been responsible for the shotgun pellets. I mean, no one is going to stand at a window expecting to be shot at.'

'She wasn't responsible. I just discovered that a young lad from the village borrowed his father's shotgun. He was shooting at birds on the roof.'

'Oh. So what are you going to do now?' Dave asked. He sounded worried. No, anxious.

'Do?' Nash queried slowly, his eyes still on the report. 'I don't know. It says here that she contacted a reporter on the Oxfordshire local paper *before* she came to view the Manor.'

'Yes, but that doesn't mean she knew you

would be here, or even that she knew the house belonged to you.'

'No,' he agreed. 'Do you have her address in Wiltshire?'

'No.'

'Don't lie,' Nash reproved without inflexion. Holding out the paper, he waited.

Dave reluctantly advanced to take it, and told him her address.

'And where's she staying in Oxford?'

He told him that as well.

'Thank you.'

'It could be Marson.'

'No, it couldn't.'

'What about the coping stone that fell?'

'What about it?'

'Marson was up there.'

'So were several other people.'

'But someone might have been killed! *She* wouldn't have wanted that.'

'No. Perhaps she was intending to push it off herself, when no one was about. Marson tripping was just bad luck.'

'And the hammer?'

'Again, easy enough to loosen. She wouldn't have been expecting Mike to take up carpentry! And she was the one who asked the carpenter to leave his tools, wasn't she?' he asked quietly. 'In case she needed to borrow something.'

'I still don't think it's her.'

'Who else is there?' He held Dave's stare, and it was the other man who looked away first.

'No need for me to stay, then, now, is there?'

'No.'

'How did you know it wasn't the property developer?' he asked as he began to stuff his belongings into a carryall.

'I went to see him.'

'And you believed him?'

'Yes.'

'He was responsible for the earlier stuff.'

'I know. You have something else you want to tell me?' he invited.

'No.' Without looking at Nash, as evasive as Phoenix had once been, he began checking round to make sure he hadn't left anything.

Slinging his bag on his shoulder, he headed for the door, and Nash asked quietly, 'Like, why?'

Dave stiffened and halted. 'What?'

'I asked you why.'

'I don't know what you mean.'

'Yes, you do.'

Dave didn't turn, didn't look at him, just stood very still. And then he did turn, gave his usual insouciant grin. Almost his usual grin. 'I really don't know what you're talking about.'

'Sabotage is what I'm talking about. Betraying a trust. Phoenix found out, didn't she?'

'You're mad.'

'No, just disappointed.' He watched the other man, grey eyes steady and direct, until Dave suddenly turned on his heel and walked out. Nash let him go. He listened to his footsteps on the bare boards and then he heard them stop. Heard them return until Dave stood in the doorway, his face a mixture of defiance and misery.

'How did you know?'

'I didn't, not for certain, not until I walked into the room just now. I had *considered* the possibility, and dismissed it, because why would someone I was employing want to rob the golden goose?'

Dave looked away. 'I tried to give you clues,' he muttered.

'Yes,' Nash agreed. And he'd been so busy thinking about Phoenix, he'd almost missed them. 'You wanted to be caught, but not to confess.'

'No,' he mumbled.

'You didn't appear greatly troubled by what you were doing.'

'Acting,' Dave said defiantly. 'You think I en-joyed cheating you? Lying to you?' he asked bitterly.

'I don't know. But Phoenix was to be the scapegoat, wasn't she? Only you found that you liked her. Who's paying you? I don't for one moment imagine it was off your own bat.'

'No. It was your ex-girlfriend.'

'Chrissie doesn't have the intelligence.'

'I know,' he said wearily. 'John Fenton put her up to it.'

'My stepbrother,' he said without surprise. He should have known. He really should have known. 'Go on,' he encouraged.

Dropping his bag with a thud at his feet, Dave leaned against the doorframe. 'I met him about a year ago. He was looking for a private detective. He knew I'd worked for you.'

'Yes,' Nash said. Because his mother had told him. With a grim smile for his own stupidity, he remembered only too clearly his mother asking him the name of the detective he'd used. 'A friend wants one,' she'd said. Because if she'd told him it was her stepson who wanted one he would never have given her Dave's name.

'I liked him at first,' Dave said tiredly. 'Seemed like a nice bloke, you know? Friendly and likeable.'

'Yes,' Nash agreed without expression. 'I know.'

'I did the job for him—just wanted someone followed, their movements noted. After that, he put a lot of business the agency's way. He liked the horses, same as I did...'

'And you got into debt,' Nash finished for him, because he'd heard it all before. If it wasn't horses, it was another kind of gambling, or some business venture that couldn't fail but always did. He'd warned his friends against John Fenton. He hadn't thought to warn Dave.

'Yeah, I got into debt. A sure thing—couldn't lose. If I didn't have enough money he'd lend it to me. Don't worry about it, pay me when you can.'

'Until the final reckoning.'

'Yes. Friendly, he was—nice, a bit embarrassed. Didn't like to ask, but he needed the money. I never even twigged,' he said disgustedly. 'He always talked about you as though you were the best thing that ever happened to him. And he hates you.'

'Yes.'

'I never found out why.'

'Neither did I,' Nash said quietly.

'I stupidly told him you'd rung me.'

'And he said he would write off your debt if you did certain things for him.'

'No,' he denied grimly, 'he used Chrissie to do that. He doesn't know I know. *She* was the one who offered me money, said she had a score to settle with you. She said she knew my name from when you'd used me.'

'I wasn't with her then.'

'I know. Fenton gave her my name. I did a bit of digging and found out that they knew each other.'

Yes, because John was always very interested in what his stepbrother got up to, in case he should ever find a lever he could use.

'I was at my wits' end, Nash. I was ruining the agency trying to pay him off. I laid off most of the staff because I couldn't afford to pay them.'

'I know.' With a grim smile, he added softly, 'Which was why I didn't suspect you. I thought you needed the money too much to ever double-cross me. But you would have had the money from me for your work here, and the money from Chrissie.'

'Yes.'

'Why didn't you come to me in the first place?'

'How the hell could I? He had me over a

bloody barrel. I *did* owe him the money.'
Straightening, he started prowling round the
room. 'You think I liked doing it? Think I en-
joyed it? You'd always played fair with me, paid
me on time. But I didn't do *all* she asked,' he
insisted, as though that might mitigate the circumstances. 'Didn't burn the place down...'

'You might have done, if I hadn't been such
a light sleeper.'

'No,' he insisted. 'If you hadn't woken up, I
would have—'

'Rescued me, become the hero? You slashed
the tyres on my car, loosened the coping stone.'

'Yes. I came up after I received your first call.
But I didn't do all I could have done,' he
pleaded. 'I exaggerated the reports, said I'd done
more damage than I had...'

'Then I suggest you go and collect your "earn-
ings" from Chrissie and pay my stepbrother off.'

'What?'

'Tell her I no longer intend to restore the
Manor. Tell her I no longer need a private detective. Tell her what you like, but in your own
best interests I *wouldn't* tell her that I know.'

'And then what?' he asked warily.

'Nothing.'

'Nothing?'

'No.'

'You aren't going to prosecute?'

'No, and if you'd come to me in the first place, I would have paid your debts and allowed you to pay me back in easy stages. Now go, before I change my mind.'

Looking bewildered, Dave collected his bag, walked to the door, then turned. 'Thank you,' he said thickly. And then he was gone. Just like Phoenix.

Nash felt betrayed, and stupid, because he should have known. But he hadn't known John knew about Chrissie. Hadn't wanted to know because Chrissie hadn't been that important. Did he know about Phoenix? Yes, of course he did, because Chrissie would have told him. Expression sharpening, galvanised into action, he chased after Dave and caught him at the front door.

Grabbing the smaller man's arm, he said with a great deal of menace, 'If anything happens to Phoenix because of any actions of yours…'

'It won't,' he denied quickly.

'Then if you value your life make sure that it doesn't. And I don't make idle threats.'

Swallowing hard, he agreed, 'I know you don't.'

'And if my stepbrother frightens you be very sure, if you cross me, I will frighten you more.'

'I won't mention her,' he said hastily.

'Or anything about her.'

'No.'

Nash nodded, and let him go. With a bitter smile, he closed the heavy front door. He, who had always prided himself on his astuteness... He should have dealt with his stepbrother a long, long time ago. Found some way to neutralise him. Perhaps it was time he had another chat with his stepfather.

Glancing at his watch, seeing it was barely seven, he walked into the room he was using and made two quick phone calls. One to his mother in Yorkshire, one to Don asking him to bring his car round.

He spent the night at a hotel on the outskirts of Harrogate, and went to see his stepfather the following morning. He then drove back through drizzling rain and leaden skies to Oxfordshire.

On Monday morning the plumber installed a Jacuzzi and finished tiling the bathroom, which was now *en suite*. The carpet-fitter came to fit the carpet in the bedroom, and the bed and bedding were delivered. He'd forgotten about curtains. Forgotten a lot of things, because his mind had been constantly on Phoenix.

When would she come?

Tuesday morning, after what should have been

a good night's sleep in a decent bed and hadn't
been, he told the builders he would be back after
lunch, just in case she came whilst he was out.
But he couldn't wait around. He thought he
would go mad.

He walked down to the village for breakfast,
then drove into Bicester to pick up some brochures on swimming pools, and returned to
Mincott Oddly in the early afternoon. He no
longer had any need to park his car at Don's.
Hoped he no longer had any need to. It was still
raining.

He asked Marson if Phoenix had been by, and,
when told that she hadn't, told him he and his
crew could leave for the day. 'You can't do much
in the rain.'

When they'd gone, wasting time, wanting it to
pass, he pushed open the double doors to the left
of the staircase into what had once been a reception room, and then through another set that led
into the east wing and what was listed as the
ballroom. The Georgians had presumably had
need of such things. He didn't. But a pool would
be nice. It would also be a selling point—if he
should sell.

Bare boards were in reasonably good condition, hairline cracks were in walls that had once
been cream and were now dingy from neglect. A

row of high windows overlooked the front, and at the end of the long room were French windows that had once opened out onto a terrace.

Mountings for chandeliers were still embedded in the high ceiling, tarnished brackets poked mournfully from the walls. With a bit of imagination he could easily picture how it had once been. Full of light and laughter, long dresses, men in knee breeches and pumps.

And then he heard a car.

Stilling, he listened, as he had listened what seemed a lifetime ago, and walked slowly to look from one of the dusty, rain-spotted windows. And smiled.

Tossing down the brochures, he walked back through the house to the front door, and opened it just as Phoenix was about to knock.

CHAPTER EIGHT

THEY looked at each other, and then she was in his arms. Face buried in her damp hair, he inhaled the scent of her shampoo. Apples, he thought. Red apples. And it felt so, so good.

'I waited until the builders had gone,' she whispered into his shoulder.

'I sent them home early. Just in case. But I was afraid you wouldn't come back.'

She hugged him, then straightened, stared up into his eyes. Releasing one hand from his back, she reached up to touch his face. 'Why didn't you tell me?' she asked softly.

'Tell you what?'

'What my father said.'

'And what did he say?'

'That if you took me away with you I would never see my parents again, that they would—disown me. And they would have done—or Dad would have done, and my mother would have been forced to obey or leave him.'

He gave a grim smile. 'Because his objective would have been achieved either way. If I'd told you, and you'd believed me, you would have been alienated from your father. If I'd taken you with me, you would have been alienated. You were eighteen years old. Your mother was crying and begging me to go... Your father wanted something better for you. You'd won a place at Oxford. He was proud of you. I had no money, not enough to keep you, help you through university.'

'But he didn't pay you to go away, did he?'

'No.'

'I'm sorry.'

'So am I. I don't know what I wanted from you, Phoenix,' he admitted honestly, 'and I don't know where it would have led if he hadn't interfered. I knew he didn't much like me...'

'I don't think it was you personally. I think he would have been the same with any young man who'd shown an interest in me.'

'Maybe, but at twenty-five, to be told I wasn't good enough for you, that I was a waster, made me extraordinarily angry. I brooded on it, magnified it, and in the end persuaded myself that it really was for the best. I'd seen friends get entangled. Marry too young... And I would have had to marry you, I think. If I'd told you, taken you away with me, I couldn't have left you to fend for yourself. There would have been money worries, babies, perhaps, struggling to survive, making compromises, and then you didn't even ask if I would be back.'

'Because I thought you'd been paid off.'

'Yes, but when I asked you to come and look at the Manor I knew none of this, and didn't understand why you were behaving as you were.'

'I wasn't the saboteur,' she denied quickly.

'I know.'

With a look of surprise on her lovely face, she queried, 'You do?'

'Yes.'

'But you *did* think it was me at one time...'

'Suspected it *could* be—and I didn't care,' he added softly, his eyes on her face. 'I was hurt, disappointed, but I wanted you.'

'It was Dave,' she confessed quietly.

'I know that too.'

'I saw him. That day we—well, in the bathroom...'

'Yes?'

'I'd walked down to the village to get some milk...'

'And stopped off for a game of baseball on the way back.' He smiled.

'You saw me?'

'Yes.'

'I didn't know.'

'I know. Go on.'

'I cut back across the field, and as I came out of the trees I saw him at the back of the Manor. He was levering out the frame of that old window, the one that was warped. The one the builder had just mended. He didn't see me, and I didn't know what to do. I was going to tell you, but then...'

'You decided I deserved all I got,' he finished for her.

'Yes. I thought it served you right, and I decided that I would use you. I would bury my emotions and just use you to satisfy myself. Only I couldn't.'

'No, because you aren't that sort of person. You felt guilty and miserable.'

'Yes, and so the next day I told Dave I'd seen him, and that if he didn't do any more I wouldn't tell you. He didn't do as much as he could have. I don't think his heart was in it. Don't punish him too severely.'

'I don't intend to punish him at all.'

'Don't you?' she asked in obvious bewilderment.

'No.'

'Why?'

'Because he was used, and he's already paid a high price for his stupidity. And I don't want to talk any more. I want to make love to you.'

Her eyes darkened, and he moved his gaze to her mouth. Her slightly parted mouth. 'I want to savour this,' he groaned as he shifted his hands to her lower back, eased her against him. 'I want it to go on for ever. I'm aroused, and hungry and aching.'

'So am I,' she managed as she prolonged the intimacy.

Holding her tighter, breathing erratic, he suddenly released her and scooped her up in his arms. Carrying her swiftly up the staircase, her arms round his neck, he took her into the newly decorated bedroom and laid her on the bed.

Eyes on her exquisite face, he perched on the edge of the bed and began to undress her. Slowly.

She reached out, her hands shaking, and began to unbutton his shirt.

When they were naked, when breathing threatened to stop their lungs altogether, they clung to each other, made love with urgent, exquisite pleasure, and then more slowly, took the time to savour each other's bodies.

Hands gentle, slightly shaking, he brushed the hair away from her face, and smiled.

'You have a beautiful smile,' she said softly.

'So do you.'

'And I'm in love with you,' she added, her eyes so very serious as she stared at him.

He closed his eyes, felt relief and happiness flow through him. 'Thank you,' he said huskily.

'For what?'

'Loving me. I want to marry you, Phoenix. Want you in my life for all time. I hadn't thought of marriage, hadn't known that was what I wanted, until you stepped from your car. No one else matters. No one else is important. I think I fell in love with you ten years ago. And I knew that I had when you stepped from your car wearing a suit too big for you.'

'I borrowed it off a friend. I didn't have anything suitable to interview the Mayoress.' Her voice was soft, husky, so serious; he felt love wash through him again.

'I've never felt like this, never wanted to protect and savour...'

'Neither have I. When we went to that hotel, it hurt so much not to be able to smile at you, talk to you, laugh, but all I could think was that my father had given you money to go away. And that you'd taken it.' Stroking one hand down his chest, then up to his chin, a tactile pleasure for them both, she said earnestly, 'My mother says she's sorry. And she is, Nash.'

'But your father always overruled any feelings she might have, didn't he?' he asked gently.

'Yes. I did love him, but he was a difficult man to know. He made the decisions and expected everyone else to comply. I'm sorry.'

Capturing her hand, he kissed her fingers. 'You haven't approved my decor.'

She smiled. 'I haven't had time.' Looking around at the oatmeal carpet and walls, the yellow, blue and green quilt, she said wryly, 'Very nice. A bit unimaginative...'

He gently slapped her. 'My mind was on other things. Are you going to marry me?'

A spark of wicked amusement in her lovely eyes, she murmured, 'Only if you let me live here.'

'You like it that much?'

'Yes.'

'I'm not having an entry hall at the back.'

She grinned. 'Why is it so warm in here?'

'Because we generate a lot of heat—and don't change the subject.' Getting to his feet, unashamedly naked, he walked across to open the window and stayed to look out over the village.

'I hope no one has binoculars trained on the house,' she teased, and he smiled.

'Don't care.'

He heard her settle herself more comfortably

on the bed behind him, and then she asked quietly, 'Why was Dave trying to sabotage the Manor?'

Turning to look at her over his shoulder, he asked in surprise, 'You didn't ask him?'

She shook her head.

Returning his attention to the view, with a rather hard light in his eyes that she couldn't see, he said quietly, 'He was being paid by my ex-girlfriend and my stepbrother.'

'John?' she exclaimed in astonishment.

Swinging round, he stared at her. 'You know him?' he demanded sharply.

Obviously puzzled by his tone, she murmured, 'I've met him. I didn't like him. But why on earth would he want to pay someone to sabotage your house? It doesn't make sense. Chrissie I could understand, but John?'

'It makes a lot of sense,' he argued grimly. '*When* did you meet him?'

'Ten years ago. Just before we split up. He came to see my father about something. What?' she demanded. '*What?*'

'Nothing.'

'Don't tell me "nothing",' she said crossly. 'You don't get a look on your face like that without it being something.' Untangling herself from the covers, she walked across to him. Searching his face, she put a gentle hand on his shoulder. 'Tell me why you're looking so grim.' When he didn't immediately answer, she added quietly, 'If we're going to be married, Nash, I shan't expect to be shut out. I had enough of that with my father. If it's your business, it's my business. I'm not like my mother. I won't be told it's none of my concern. You *are* my concern. As I'm yours.'

Reaching for her, he held her warm body against him. 'Yes. I'm sorry. If John went to see your father then it was for one reason only. To tell him I was no good. And *that* was why your father behaved as he did.' With a hollow laugh, he murmured, 'And I should have known. I should have known then, and I should have known now. Busy, busy John. Naive of me, but I'd no idea that John even knew about you ten years ago, let alone where you lived. He would have smiled,' he continued, 'because he smiles so very well. Been charming, believable, apologetic. "I anguished and anguished," he might have said, and probably did, "over whether I should come and see you, Mr Langrish, but I think you ought to know what sort of man my brother is." Because he calls me his brother,' he murmured, 'never stepbrother.' Looking down, he searched her still face. 'He's charming and likeable, vitally attractive—and totally flawed.'

Gently kissing his mouth, she urged, 'Go on. You never mentioned your family when we were together.'

'No. My father died when I was five and my mother brought me up on her own until I was sixteen. And then she met Peter, a widower with a fifteen-year-old son. I was really pleased. I thought it would be nice to be a family again. John seemed nice, friendly, helpful, and as pleased about the arrangement as I was. But they lived in Yorkshire and we lived in Kent. I was in the middle of exams, John was just about to start his, and so, when they got married, I stayed with a friend during the week, so as not to interrupt my schooling, and went up to Yorkshire for weekends and holidays. And every time I was home money would go missing from my mother's purse, jewellery, things from Peter's study. Everything was found in my bedroom—apart from the money.'

'And they accused you.'

'No, no one accused. That was what was so awful. Peter looked mortally hurt, my mother upset, and John was sympathetic. Kind. My mother knew it wasn't me, but she loved Peter...'

'And accusing his son would have made things awkward for her?'

'Not only awkward. Thwarted, John is vicious.

He didn't—doesn't—like my mother. He wouldn't have liked anyone who married his father. Peter is extremely wealthy and John is paranoid that he will leave his money away from his son. And I was equally determined that my mother would not suffer. After all those years of struggle, managing on her own, she deserved to be happy. And so I made a pact with John. He would leave my mother alone, and I would stay away.'

'But you were *sixteen*.'

'Yes. I told them I didn't like living in Yorkshire, that all my friends were in Kent, and so an arrangement was made with the friend I was staying with. Mike,' he murmured.

'The Mike who's your architect?'

'Mmm. Peter paid rent for my upkeep until I was able to stand on my own two feet. My mother would come down to see me. We would go out for lunch, the cinema, whatever—and she felt so wretchedly guilty. Still does.'

'And you reassure her, pretend it doesn't matter.'

'Mmm.'

'You still meet?'

'Of course. She comes down for a few days two or three times a year.'

'And you aren't even bitter, are you?' she asked, a look of gentle surprise on her face.

'Bitter? No. I like my stepfather, and I respect him, and I certainly didn't blame him for taking his son's side above mine. John was always very careful not to let his father see what he's like. I don't know why he hates me so much, just that he does.'

'And does Peter still not know what his son is like?'

'He knows, but I advised him, for everyone's safety, not to let his son know that he knew. When he finally found out, he was going to alter his will. I persuaded him not to.'

'Because if he cuts him off John might do something—stupid?'

'Yes. But now there's you to consider, and I won't have you put at risk. I went up to see my stepfather at the weekend.'

'And told him what?'

'What his son has been up to.'

'And?'

'And now there is a codicil to his will saying that if John does anything threatening to *anyone*, but specifically to either you or me, when he dies, Peter's money will go to charity. John will be thoroughly investigated before any money is handed over. And John will be told that.'

'What about your mother?'

'She's already provided for. Peter is extremely wealthy.'

'How absolutely wretched,' she said sadly. 'Is he jealous of you, do you think?'

'I don't know, although my staff certainly think so.' He smiled. 'Because I refuse to allow him access to any of my businesses. My friends kindly say nothing when I warn them not to have anything to do with him. He seems to have no morals, no concept of right from wrong, and he's ruined more people than I care to count.'

'Dangerous.'

'Yes, because you never know what he will do. He tried to ruin me several times, and when that didn't work he ruined several of my friends instead. Dave stupidly got into debt to him. John knew Chrissie, presumably knew we had split up, and told her how she could get back at me. She employed Dave to sabotage the Manor.'

'I'm so sorry. I liked Dave.'

'So did I.' Smoothing her hair back so that he could see her perfect face, he asked, 'Why didn't you like John? Most people do...in the beginning.'

'I don't know. Just something about him that grated. Anyway, I was in love with you.'

'Were you?'

'Yes.'

'And now?'

'Now?' she queried with a frown. 'I already told you how I feel.'

'And you haven't changed your mind?'

'Because of John, do you mean?' And when he nodded she shook her head. 'You don't get rid of me so easily. Not this time.'

'I don't want to get rid of you.' The church clock struck the hour, and he stilled.

'What time is it?' he asked urgently.

She lifted her wrist and gave a foolish smile, because, of course, she didn't have anything on. Her watch had been removed along with everything else. 'Why do you need to know the time? Bored with me already?'

'No, but I have to see the vicar.'

'To arrange our wedding?' she asked hopefully, and he smiled.

'That's a thought, but no. I promised to go and visit him. On *your* instructions.'

'I didn't tell you to go and visit the vicar,' she laughed.

'No, but you told me to be nice to the villagers. Why?' he asked gently. 'Why is it so important to them that I stay? To bring wealth to the village?'

'Partly, I expect, but mostly because of stability and tradition. So many villages are dying, young people moving away to the towns. With the Manor occupied, with work being generated, staff…'

'Staff?' he exclaimed. 'I'm now to have *staff*?'

She giggled. Hugged him. 'You'll love it, really you will.'

'No, I won't. I work from London.'

Eyes dancing, she told him, 'You can commute.'

'I don't want to commute.'

'Live in London in the week, then, and here at weekends.'

'I'm not leaving you here on your own in the week,' he protested.

'The villagers will look after me. But not at first,' she added softly. 'At first I shall want to be with you in London. But when the babies come along…'

'*Babies?*'

'Don't you want babies?' she asked innocently.

'It doesn't seem to be a question of what *I* want…'

She grinned again, began to inscribe little circles on his chest. 'It doesn't, does it? Do we have time to make love again before we have to see the vicar?'

'We? I don't recall inviting *you*.'

'New policy,' she murmured naughtily. 'I no longer wait to be invited. Why haven't you got any wardrobes?'

'Because I'm waiting for them to be delivered. But I do have a Jacuzzi.'

'Very historically accurate! Is it working?'

'Mmm-hmm.'

'Good.' Releasing herself, she took his hand. 'Through here?'

'Mmm.'

She opened the door to the bathroom, gave an enchanting smile and a nod of approval, and tugged him across to the Jacuzzi. He didn't need much tugging.

New towels were lined up along the heated towel rail, and she reached out to feel their softness as she walked past them. 'Nice,' she praised.

'Mmm.'

'Which levers do I press?' she asked as she halted at the sunken Jacuzzi.

'All of them?'

Her smile widened—and he fell in love with her all over again. But if they stayed he would need to warn the village about his stepbrother, he thought sombrely. There would be no chances taken with Phoenix's safety. No chances at all.

He wondered how she would feel about having a minder. No, he knew how she would feel, and so he didn't tell her.

'What's wrong?' she whispered.

'Nothing.'

'Then why are you looking so serious?'

'Because love is a serious business. And I love you so very much.'

'That sounded glib.'

Gathering her into his arms, he said seriously, 'It might have sounded it, but every word was meant.' Straightening, he forced a smile. Reaching out, he pulled one of the levers and water gushed into the bath. He pulled another one, and it began to bubble.

'Oh, and by the way,' he said as he suddenly remembered something—although why gushing water should have reminded him he had no idea. 'I discovered why someone covered up your bar tracery.'

She looked absolutely delighted. 'Really? Why?'

'Because when the sun goes down it shines right through that window and blinds anyone coming in the front door.'

She stared at him for a moment, her eyes wide, and then she gave a slow smile, an infectious chuckle. 'Then they shouldn't have moved the staircase and put the front door at the back of the house, should they?'

He laughed. 'You wretch,' he said softly. 'You little wretch. I walked right into that one, didn't I?'

'I would say so, yes. And the water seems to be ready.' Releasing him, one hand on his shoulder to steady herself, she stepped down into the bath. 'Coming in?'

'Yes, Phoenix. I'm coming in.' Stepping purposefully in beside her, he picked her up and dumped her gently in the water.

'Don't get my hair wet,' she yelled. 'I didn't bring my hairdrier.'

'Too late,' he said with monumental satisfaction as she came up dripping. 'You can't have *everything* your own way.' Settling himself beside her, he pulled her into his arms. And kissed her.

Hair plastered to her head, lashes spiky, laughter in her lovely eyes, she whispered, 'That *was* my way.'

'Good.' Eyes warm and full of love, he kissed her wet mouth.

They were a bit late meeting with the vicar.

**Remember the magic of the film
It's a Wonderful Life?
The warmth and tender emotion of
Truly, Madly, Deeply?
The feel-good humor of *Heaven Can Wait?***

Well, even if we can't promise you angels that look like
Alan Rickman or Warren Beatty, starting in June in
Harlequin Romance®, we can promise a brand-new
miniseries: GUARDIAN ANGELS. Featuring all of your
favorite ingredients for a perfect novel: great heroes,
feisty heroines and a breathtaking romance—all with a
celestial spin.

Look for Guardian Angels in:

June 1998: THE BOSS, THE BABY AND THE BRIDE (#3508)
by Day Leclaire

August 1998: HEAVENLY HUSBAND (#3516)
by Carolyn Greene

October 1998: A GROOM FOR GWEN (#3524)
by Jeanne Allan

December 1998: GABRIEL'S MISSION (#3532)
by Margaret Way

**Falling in love sometimes needs a little help
from above!**

Available wherever Harlequin books are sold.

FIVE STARS
MEAN SUCCESS

If you see the "5 Star Club" flash on a book,
it means we're introducing you to one of our
most STELLAR authors!

Every one of our Harlequin and Silhouette
authors who has sold over 5 MILLION BOOKS
has been selected for our "5 Star Club."

We've created the club so you won't miss
any of our bestsellers. So, each month
we'll be highlighting every original book within
Harlequin and Silhouette written by our
bestselling authors.

NOW THERE'S NO WAY ON EARTH OUR STARS WON'T BE SEEN!

5 STAR CLUB
AUTHOR

HARLEQUIN®   Silhouette®

P5STAR

MEN at WORK

All work and no play? Not these men!

April 1998
KNIGHT SPARKS by Mary Lynn Baxter

Sexy lawman Rance Knight made a career of arresting the bad guys. Somehow, though, he thought policewoman Carly Mitchum was framed. Once they'd uncovered the truth, could Rance let Carly go...or would he make a citizen's arrest?

MEN IN UNIFORM

May 1998
HOODWINKED by Diana Palmer

CEO Jake Edwards donned coveralls and went undercover as a mechanic to find the saboteur in his company. Nothing— or no one—would distract him, not even beautiful secretary Maureen Harris. Jake had to catch the thief—*and* the woman who'd stolen his heart!

MEN OF STEEL

June 1998
DEFYING GRAVITY by Rachel Lee

Tim O'Shaughnessy and his business partner, Liz Pennington, had always been close—but never *this* close. As the danger of their assignment escalated, so did their passion. When the job was over, could they ever go back to business as usual?

TALL, DARK AND SMART E=MC

MEN AT WORK™

Available at your favorite retail outlet!

 HARLEQUIN®   Silhouette®

Harlequin Romance®

Delightful

Affectionate

Romantic

Emotional

Tender

Original

Daring

Riveting

Enchanting

Adventurous

Moving

Harlequin Romance—the
series that has it all!

HROM-G